# THE PEDESTAL

*Books by George Lanning*

THE PEDESTAL
THIS HAPPY RURAL SEAT
TECHNIQUE IN FICTION
(with Robie Macauley)

# THE
# PEDESTAL

## GEORGE LANNING

**HARPER & ROW, PUBLISHERS**
*New York*

LIBRARY OF CONGRESS CATALOG CARD NUMBER: 66-15739

C-Q

For my dear aunt
ROSE LANNING

# THE PEDESTAL

# 1

THESE LAST nights, dark has come on the boom of wings. The owls are back, exploding out of the woods below us and from the line of trees along the river. Their barking evokes an image of wolves—though I've never heard a wolf and I suppose bark is the wrong word for the noise they make. But the analogy, if incorrect, is expressive of the sense we both have of something dangerous and vital in the country night, something we are being warned to keep away from. Death there, or at least a fierce indignity; eyes there, all coldly judging. Talons there, and beak.

This house is far too big for us, but I have always loved it and even Eleanor enjoys its size—if not always its isolation. My grandfather built it when a place with twenty-five or -eight rooms cost about what the newest prefab down in the valley cost the year before last. Of course it's an eyesore, if you've got that kind of eye. But both of us like space, doors to close, corridors to walk along, stairs to climb. And, because my family has always had a good deal of money, the house has never been allowed to deteriorate, though it's been occupied only for short periods since my grandmother's death in 1949—and even in her time was seldom open for more than two months a year. It was intended for vacations with the whole family present, and then for retirement; but my grandfather dropped dead one day in his office, and my grandmother lived on in her big, sunny Cleveland house on a bluff above Edgewater Drive because she adored the city spread wide across the harbor from her and hated the idea of being alone on a hillside where the boom of wings celebrates the coming of the night.

We are only about seven hundred feet back from the road, but the property is screened by Norway pines my grandfather set out just before he died, when what had been scarcely more than a country lane became the principal route between the highway town to the west of us and Oldchurch, the hilltop village to our east. People used to go to Oldchurch to "take the air" on the porch of a small wooden hotel built in the 1850s; now they go to take the very good liquor and food at the very good restaurant that came into being about eight years ago. Or to stay at the new lodge where the minimum charge for a double in season is $36 a day. We bless those pines—four rows of them, magnificently tall—for they cut off the dust and, to some extent, the noise of Jaguars, Lincolns, Cadillacs, and Mercedes racing past. This was an unknown country when my grandfather found it; today it has at least a semblance of fame in ads and brochures: piedmont country, leaning up against the Alleghenies. My father was offered a quarter of a million for the property last winter. There are a little over twelve acres: pines to the front, a grove of them on one side, the forest of hardwoods below, and— beyond a dirt road—the river holding. Space for any number of motels and roadhouses. This grand old bare-floored house would be torn down, of course, the pedestal kicked out with the rest of the junk. There would be stories about the place for a while, as there have always been, but eventually the cutting down of all the trees, the division of the estate into small parcels, would mix the taletellers up about what had ostensibly happened where.

I have no desire to live long enough to see any of this—except the pedestal's destruction. Eleanor, on the other hand, enjoys shuddering at the general prospect: she sees us as the grand family in the great house, vulgar commercialization creeping toward it. A favorite books of hers is Louis Bromfield's *The Green Bay Tree;* I suspect that the mansion in that novel, imperiled by industry in the valley below, seems to dramatize our own situation—and to console at the same time, since whatever vulgarity we may eventually be confronted with will be as invincibly picturesque as what we have already.

Such a comfortable threat, indeed; the more delightful because it can never come to anything without our consent.

I am less certain about the threat the pedestal offers. And it has already received our consent, for we two brought it here. I can't talk to Eleanor, though it could be important to find out what she knows or guesses. Sarah guesses something, without any question, but I am almost certain that she looks on me as the pedestal's agent.

As, perhaps, I am.

# 2

WHEN WE bought it, some of our friends told us we were crazy—should have been paid to haul it away. We found it in a river town about sixty miles south of here, farther into the hills and approachable by no very good roads, so that the trip took over two hours. The pedestal was a minor item in the contents of an enormous house of immense architectural distinction which was soon to be torn down. Most of the furniture was borax or bad nineteenth century—one wondered how a family capable of the brilliance of the house could have been so indifferent to its interior; but just as I tugged at Eleanor's arm, whispering we'd got the long drive back and ought to go, the pedestal was carried onto the platform. We'd been through the house earlier, while the sale was in that stage familiar to all backwoods auction-goers, when lusterware and coin glass, Rockingham earthenware, and surely the sixty-millionth set of Haviland in this state alone sell for outrageous prices, and I didn't remember seeing the pedestal any place. And we'd even peered in closets, followed stray flights of steps up to odd little rooms. Nevertheless, there it was, magnificent:

just over six feet tall (so that one had the absurd sense it ought to have been taking bids on the small auctioneer), solid of stem, broad of base, supported on three diminutive clawed feet. The wood gleamed a rich blood-brown in the declining afternoon sun—where in God's name had these commonplace people used it? I looked at some of the other stuff to be sold or standing around me already bid on: the split down the middle harvest table of doubtful cherry; the woebegone Victorian parlor chairs with two out of four china casters gone; the corner cupboard without brasswork and with sadly warped shelves; the lumpy, pseudo-Federal sofa with chipped veneer. The pedestal was beautiful, and real.

We made a single bid—and got it. Triumphantly, for five dollars; but I think we could have bought it even for less: fifty cents, maybe. Where had its owners used it? Where, more to the present point, would anybody else use it? Obviously, it was designed to serve as the focal point in a long room, the central object in a "vista," something to be approached. It would be absurd even in a big room unless the ceiling was quite high. Our place at Owl Hill was its predestined home. We at once imagined it standing in the living room against the bank of sliding windows that opens onto the west terrace: eminent, darkly gleaming, the light of that wall of glass behind it, supporting on its broad top . . . What?

"An urn," said Eleanor tentatively, on the drive home. "Or that awful bust of Dante I found in the basement. Except we don't want a permanent joke, do we? A candelabra?"

"Brum," I said, my eyes on the twisting, steeply descending road.

"Yes. Brum. Just one, anyway, if that means just one. Though, with candles . . . I mean, how would we ever get up to light them?"

"That's something we wouldn't be doing every evening."

"I still think an urn might . . . Except it would need to be such an important urn, wouldn't it?—or else dripping ivy, which I'd have to keep hauling in the stepladder to water."

"Let Sarah."

"Sarah hates heights. She won't even go out on the kitchen porch to shake the duster. When I send her down to the pool, she uses the basement door. Haven't you noticed all the gray fluff over the rhododendrons in front? She actually empties the vacuum on them! No, not ivy, I guess."

So, comfortably, we talked our way home, the great pedestal lolling inert, unconscious but alive it almost seemed, in the back seat, its three little claws poking out through the window.

# 3

OWL HILL is a name without the usual exaggeration or optimism. We are near the eastern end of a narrow, wooded ridge some five miles long. Just beyond our property line the road swings down into the valley that separates us from Oldchurch hill. Our land, running south off the road, descends gently as far as the front of the house, but it begins there to fall away noticeably, and the back—from which the kitchen porch protrudes—is high in the air. On below, my grandfather had terraces made at intervals: one for the tennis court, one for the garages, one for a small, formal garden surrounded by boxwood, one for a good-sized swimming pool. Beyond these terraces the trees begin: pin oaks, rock maples, sycamores, walnuts, enormous dogwoods, and the exotic-leaved tulips. The going is steep though not exacting, and the way is studded with large boulders that make excellent seats for adults and superb Indian lookouts for children. Bounding the hillside at its base is a brick wall covered with trumpet vines and wisteria and roses. A door opens onto the dirt road which parallels the road at the top of the ridge, and across the way is a door in another brick wall which gives access to the land we own along the river. There isn't much down there except for a concrete pavilion, regularly flooded in the spring, which the family has used for impromptu picnics, small, informal dances, and no doubt a certain amount of surreptitious lovemaking and skin-partying. The river is narrow and usually quite shallow where it passes our property, and the most interesting sight it provides is that of an occasional great blue heron fishing with a total absorption. There are bass to be caught farther on; not here. Once in a while, at night, we can see the lights of the frog fishermen moving along the banks. Beyond the river the land rises steeply, and is heavily forested and innocent for some distance of any structure other than Hilltop, an Episcopal mission which serves as a place of recreation and occasional prayer for two adults and ten children. Most of the local people are Church of Christ or Adventist, and want nothing to do with the boozy, smart-aleck crowd that turns up at St. Peter's-in-the-Valley during summer months and holiday weekends (the mission, a fairly familiar kind of Anglican error, is St. Peter's sop not so much to ecumenicity as to the local chamber of commerce).

As you may have guessed, that crowd from St. Peter's, which changes substantially with the seasons, constitutes most of our local acquaintance, except for the ten or twelve families in the town west of us, and a few people in Oldchurch village, who are the quality folk in the county. The types of these people used to send Eleanor and me into gales of laughter—and meanly we shared our amusement with our "real" friends at home in Cleveland. The fact is, of course, that you can't live in a place for any length of time and go on seeing your neighbors as caricatures. Some, we found, we liked very much; others we could tolerate. Others we disliked for reasons that were simply human: a mutual antipathy that had nothing to do with education or background or sensibility.

A thing that amazed us—until we, too, began to feel the fascination—was the encyclopedic knowledge that the people we knew possessed about everyone else: not merely colleagues and friends. They were brilliantly informed about the life of our rural route mail carrier, about the Oldchurch postmaster, about the man who repairs everyone's car, about the cleaning women who move weekly through our houses, about the reformed alcoholic who does so many families' yards. The amount of incest, adultery, abortion, bestiality, drunkenness we were told of quite assaulted our city-innocent ears. Our friend Ray Gravatt said, "Before I came here, I thought I'd run into almost every kind of depravity or weakness. After all, I'd served in a couple of pretty rough in-city parishes. But most of our sinners were Episcopalians. I just didn't know what went on in some of the more fundamentalist groups."

# 4

THE PEDESTAL was of such awkward dimensions that it took both of us to get it into the house—as it had into the car. Neither of us, I think, felt winded, but by the time we'd lifted it out, up the steps and across the porch, through the door and down the hall into the living room, we found it impossible to sustain an even flow of speech. Thus, I was some moments realizing that Eleanor wanted to leave the thing on its side for the present. "To clean," she panted; "oil . . . it. Hasn't been . . . years, looks sif. Spider eggs, bottom."

So it was as something recumbent that the pedestal gave me, some time later, the first unpleasant shock. We were due at the Cardens' in just under an hour, allowing even for the very late entrance permissible at a big cocktail party. Bumping the great mass to the floor before the terrace windows, we made for the shower—actually, I shower while Eleanor floats around my feet, tickling my ankles with her toes (we have old-fashioned plumbing here, no glass-lined separate cubicles). We achieved the almost-impossible and managed to arrive at the Cardens' exactly forty minutes later, though they live ten miles north of us in Royalton Court House. All of the bores, who generally come first to parties, had left or were on the verge, and very soon only the hard core of hell-this-is-Saturday-night were still there. I fell in with these happy souls rather too enthusiastically, for the Cardens themselves, despite their magnificently bold concrete and steel vacation "hideaway" (twelve rooms), are the early-arrival sort, and one does what one must to suffer their hospitality. The result, of course, was that I got thoroughly drunk and had to lie down for a while before I felt enough in control to get the two of us back home. And that led to the fight. Eleanor doesn't drive although, since she drinks less than I do, it would be to the advantage of both of us if she'd get a license. But she believes that the male has total responsibility for the family car (obviously, we are a one-car family, however unfashionable that may be today). Her conviction would be absurd if we didn't have so much money. As it is, she calls taxis or hires cars and drivers when I'm unavailable. Given the way Eleanor's mind works, it may be that she sees this arrangement as far more indicative of our standing than a mere second car, however costly. But it has its marked inconveniences, and this night was an example. She'd wanted to go home a couple of hours earlier, but during this time I'd been first resistant and then unavailable. She was not in a forgiving mood, and on that long, dark drive back we quarreled bitterly. All of the hostilities that build up in any marriage came boiling out once again. That I'd been ill, that my illness had driven us to get out of the city and settle down in this god-forsaken landscape of hills and woods and people like the Cardens—*and* the damned owls, *and* the frightening darkness . . . She went on and on. Naturally, she wound back to the fact that we were childless after six years of marriage. What was there between us? Was there anything enduring? I wanted to say: Think how happy we were today, driving to the auction, getting that beautiful bargain pedestal, driving home again. I wanted to say: There wasn't time this afternoon, there in the bathtub, but remember how much fun we have, think of tomorrow. . . . Of course, she'd have said, I'll never take a bath with you again—and, though she would, I'd have been assessed some heavy penalties first. So I said nothing and drove like vengeance down the empty country roads. It was a moony night, and tree shadows lay across our pale way; in the near distance farmhouses loomed startlingly out of perspective. There was an occasional dark crossing of wings. Her voice gets so shrill when she's angry; an ugly voice. She hurt me and I hated her; I didn't answer a word. I loved her too, even then, but once it crossed my mind that if she didn't watch herself I might love the memory of her more.

Going into our place, I wheeled the big car too close to the left-hand gatepost and there was an ominous grating noise. That finished us. Eleanor, announcing that she wouldn't drive with me again until whatever had happened had been fixed, was off and away the minute I stopped in the oval before our steps. She'd crossed the porch and gone into the house before I'd undone my safety belt and got out to look for the worst. The worst turned out to be a deeply scratched front fender and a curious crumpling of the metal covering over the rocker panel. I meditated upon these for a little time, feeling incapable of any more positive action, and then I wobbled around the front of the car and up the steps to the door. By now I was thoroughly drunk again; I'd brought us safely back, the checks in my mind were all released, and I wanted a little comfort for our bitter talk, for the whole boring, disastrous evening. A light was on just within, and I made a wavering progress to the hall's farther end, where a doorway leads to our living room and one of our strategically scattered bars. What I had to have was a drink.

What I got, initially, was a shock that temporarily restored sobriety. Moonlight flooded in through the terrace windows, and prone on the floor just within them lay what seemed to be a body: grotesquely outfitted with a ruff and minus its head. I was a full minute realizing that this was the pedestal, and the ruff merely the ornamental section surrounding its top. My hand still trembling, I advanced into the room and put on a table lamp. The moonlight receded; the windows turned black; and the pedestal shone dully. I heard the rush of wings as something, startled, flew off the terrace toward the nighttime woods. Far away an owl made a gobbling call, and out on the road a late last car sped by.

How like a body it was: too long, too large in some places, small in others, yet withal, in the faint illumination, convincing in a nightmare way that an actual body mightn't have been. One of the claw feet caught the light, as if the great mass had slightly shifted—and I almost had to assure myself that I'd simply failed to notice the reflection there before.

# 5

"No, DEFINITELY not an urn," said Eleanor the next morning. Rags, water pan, and oil bottle beside her, she was giving the pedestal a thorough going-over (the vacuum off to one side had, presumably, swallowed the spiders' eggs). "I think it grew in the night," she went on cheerfully—the kind of determined cheerfulness she often assumes after one of our bad quarrels. All is to be ignored, though all is remembered with clarity and in minute detail. And will be trotted out in small amounts for months to come—a letting off of the poisons in harmless amounts, as one of her—or my—many advisers has put it, which does you good without starting everything up again.

"It nearly scared the life out of me," I answered, trying for her tone. "Last night, I mean. I came in here and in the dark it looked like a body."

"Candles are out, too," she went on—this, intended as an answer, was meant to distract me from whatever morbid thoughts I was having. That a more natural response might have worked better was something neither she nor the professionals seemed capable of realizing. She dipped her rag in the water, added oil, and began vigorously to polish one of the claw feet. "Horrid things," she said gaily. "Tap tap, scratch scratch . . . where will my little feet go?" She felt obliged to laugh. "But, really, aren't they absurdly small to bear the weight of a thing like this? And what are they supposed to be, do you think? Look." She traced the pattern with her rag. "Is that fur or a vine leaf or a mad abstraction of an acanthus? Except it'd be odd to put toenails on an acanthus or a vine leaf, wouldn't it? Or wouldn't it?" Groaning, hand clasped to back and knees cracking, she got up. "Help me to raise it, Johnny. I've done as much as I can for the present. I'll get Sarah to oil it again in a day or so—it absolutely needs to be *fed* with oil: you see how the surface is already beginning to come back?"

So we raised it, and a mighty thing did it seem we'd done: a temple pillar, a god found in rubble, now restored to sinister eminence. But at the time, naturally, I told myself that the "sinister" was subjective, a result of moonlight and drink and disordered emotions. It was just a five-dollar piece of wonderful junk we'd found at a small-town auction. And that's right, surely that's right—for now, the moment I write this down, I don't hear a thing. Yet, supposing it doesn't move tonight, supposing I persuade myself it's never moved, there'll still be one puzzle I'll never solve: how, in our exhaustive tour of that old house, we missed it. Where did it lurk against the invader? Along what corridor did it slowly tiptoe, seeking its rightful claimants?

"We'll wait and brood," said Eleanor, stepping back and looking at the pedestal appraisingly. "What goes on top must be the child of inspiration."

# 6

THAT WAS one of Sarah's days—she came three times a
week, and now and again in the evening to wait at table
when we had people for dinner. Sarah was the sort of massive woman who always looks to be boiling and heaving
with rage at the latest injustice done to her, and in fact she
often was. But, except for her fear of heights (which elim-
inated window washing and wallpaper cleaning), she was
both fast and good—and, what I think recommended her
most of all to Eleanor, an unfailing source of local news.
We discussed her revelations with awe: our dinners on
Sarah's days generally lasted longer than on other days as
Eleanor took me story by story through surrounding
households. It is a fact that an accomplished talebearer, as
Sarah was, can persuade one to believe almost anything,
even when the story centers on people one knows quite
well and sees in a way that Sarah never sees them. At first,
before she got into the spirit of things, Eleanor had tried to
correct some of Sarah's "facts," but the effect was to turn
up the boiler and start the heaving, and so after a time she
simply kept silence and, when Sarah momentarily subsided,

prodded her with a casual "I suppose everything's all right now between the . . . ?" Of course, it never was, and Sarah was the one who knew. We told each other that what we appreciated was the power of Sarah's rhetoric, but in fact we found that on occasion her tales subtly colored our opinion of one person or another. And every so often she proved to be exactly right, and we entirely wrong, which further confused our general view of her reliability. She did two other households, and presently we found out that all of us possessed approximately the same body of horrendous knowledge. It made a curious bond: a name would come up at a party, a reference be made to a particular event, and our glances would swivel toward one another, an implicit nod in the exchange, and we would try not to smile at the innocence of the speaker.

Sarah's stories were always appalling. In the world she inhabited (she was the wife of a local farmer who worked part-time grading township roads; to a degree, he served as her legman) civility was almost unknown, kindness was merely the absence of brutality, and loyalty was a quality peculiar to the family dog. It was a world so devoid of the elementary decencies that at first the very sight of her depressed me. Had she lived in a tenement, or a shack of the kind that one can find back in the hills, I suppose I'd have regarded her as so rare an exotic as to have no connection with ordinary human life. But in fact she lived in her husband's family home, an honest, roomy, foursquare house which they had done over a few years before at considerable expense (we had once been invited to inspect the all-electric kitchen, so much superior to our own, and then had had Hawaiian punch with gin in it on the front porch). Both of them had cars, their daughters—if only in the nick

—were married and settled in prosperous homes of their own, they went to the American Legion lodge on Saturday nights and danced and got tight, and they were considering buying a second home in Florida. Then: why this catastrophic world vision? I can't find an answer, or bundle of answers, that seems adequate. I can only say that the country life brings out all of the soul's latent ferocity and opens dampers on fires one didn't know were smoldering. The lyricism of spring, in the country, is a song about hatred. And summer hums of ripeness and death.

In time, then, I found that Sarah's outlook and my outlook were at least in partial accord. And of course in any society it is consoling to believe the worst about one's friends, and disagreeable to think better of them than one thinks of oneself.

As the relationship between Eleanor and me deteriorated, I suppose that both of us found Sarah more and more of a comfort. If she never quite confirmed our worst opinions of those we knew, she somehow assured us that at least they were as wretched as we.

# 7

Eleanor claimed, now and again, that the trouble with us was that we weren't prepared for marriage. Since I was thirty-three at the time and Eleanor thirty-one, I felt that we should have been about as well prepared as any two people could be. Sociologists, those exquisite comedians, have a fancy name for marriages between unequals, and my impression is that in general they don't regard such unions as good risks. But I don't think they've given much attention to the marriages of equals—social equals, anyway; and that was our particular situation. Eleanor's father is chairman of a bank and director of forty-odd corporations; his father before him directed what was for the time an equivalent number of companies. In short, she was every bit as good as I was, and our two families were squarely behind us. More, we had the same tastes and a similar cultivation of them, and complementary differences: she liked to cook (some of the time) and ran a house excellently, and I liked tools, restoring furniture, and working in the garden. She could appreciate the beauty of an old chest taken down to the wood and stripped of its hardware-store brasswork, and I liked an immaculate living room with flowers in bowls on tables and lamps lighted and the golden glint of cocktails in Waterford glasses. And, yes, we got along fine in bed. Bed and bathtub and sometimes out in the woods and even, for kicks, in the car now and then.

So how weren't we prepared for marriage?—or as prepared as anybody can be? It was plain we weren't, said Eleanor, because we couldn't make a baby. We'd both had the whole range of tests, and there wasn't any physiological reason why we couldn't have a kid every eleven months. A couple of years ago, Eleanor'd persisted in telling our friends about the problems of the "infertile woman," a boring phrase out of one of those upchucking female magazines that even the brightest women read. Since my last illness—the one mercy it had offered me—she'd said far less; but I wished when she did bring up the subject it was not always in a spirit of recrimination. I, too, badly wanted a child.

Have you a sense of us now? I've had the experience of trying to read narratives in which I couldn't for the life of me make out the characters. And so, pretty soon, I lost interest. I like people standing on real ground, leaning against real walls. I want to know what they are, who they are. I have no interest in the anonymous everyman. You have a vague idea of our house, I hope, and of our society. You don't, I realize, know how the two of us look. And no more do I. We're the blue-eyed people of the recessive gene that geneticists say is receding too far; but there are still plenty of us around—around country club pools, at least, and the livelier parties. And it's a fact that the brown-eyes often make over us. So I suppose we're something vanishing, and that the brown-eyed people regard us as valuable enough to be appreciated in the here and now. We are also tow-haired—and tow, unlike blond, stubbornly resists darkening. We glitter like bright metal, in sun or lamplight, as our friends turn gray. And our legs are long. How do we look? You know as much as I do, now. Like the privileged extinct. That's close enough.

# 8

It was two or three nights after our quarrel that I first heard the pedestal walk. Eleanor and I were again on genuinely peaceful terms, but the skin was still tender, and our bodies avoided one another in bed as our eyes skipped sideways during the day, dreading the straight-on look that might reveal too much—or, more terribly, nothing. For the last few weeks I'd been having trouble getting to sleep; getting up in the morning at a respectable hour. Since I had nothing to do at Owl Hill except, in the doctors' phrase, to compose and refresh myself, I'd tried to keep to a regular schedule: up by nine, bed by midnight. In the long, dragging hours between I read, took my sprayer and went down into the woods in search of the ubiquitous poison ivy, cut up windfalls for the fireplaces, spent hours bathing in the nude or lying nude in the sun (dreaming pornographic dreams), drove up and down graveled country roads, and then—but seldom before five—headed back to the house for the first drink of the day. I had got to the point where I even enjoyed our twice-a-week excursion to a supermarket in the town west of us. I would squeeze a head of lettuce as if it were a Vegas whore. I was dizzy with the whole social, sexy event: all the women looked good, and those sheltering bays of canned milk in six-packs, lightbulbs in cartons, offered just the right places for amiable transactions. Small wonder that any party, even a dull one, got me wound up—every party was a potential big-time A&P. Somewhere, I kept thinking, I'd meet the One who'd turn me really on, resolve me for myself, discover my promise, exalt my ego, love me forever, and never ask boring questions. Jesus, I was tired of the way things were, of the daily sapping away of the good will and fine feeling that I thought I met the world with until I was told otherwise.

I suppose all of these thoughts—these adolescent restlessnesses and sick hostilities, if you will—were boiling around in my mind that particular night. Anyway, I couldn't sleep, I was so full of rage and boredom. Finally, I arranged myself flat on my back (if you are troubled with insomnia, an article I'd read had suggested, find a comfortable position and *do not move from it until you've counted at least to five hundred*). I began to *breathe deeply*—twenty-eight, twenty-nine, thirty—and *exhale slowly* (a sure combatant of sleeplessness, another article had said). And what would I think about—fifty-six, fifty-seven—since thinking was my trouble? Sixty. *Play games in your mind*, another expert advised. If you are "literary," try to remember as many titles as you can by an especially prolific author: Hugh Walpole, say, or Kathleen Norris. Seventy-four, seventy-five. Or choose a color—green, black, red—and set yourself the task of recalling all of the book titles in which that color appears. Eighty-one, eighty-two. From experience I avoided green and red, which are—ninety—booby-trapped (is *The Green Years* a fair inclusion, for instance?). Black was always good, but—ninety-eight, ninety-nine, one hundred—too easy. I gave up counting at this point and settled, as so often before, on blue: *A Pair of Blue Eyes, The Blue Cloak, The Blue Shadow Mystery, The Return of Blue-Mask, Blue Water, The Blue Horse of Taxco* . . . I'd just got to the point where I was debating the admission of *The Turquoise Shop* when I heard a sound in the room below. In the spring country quiet, in that bare-floored, high-ceilinged house, it was quite distinct: at first I thought a window was being forced up—a window that hadn't been raised in a long time and had grown to its frame. But below us was the living room: the glass wall along the terrace slides open quite silently; the windows are casement. In fact, windows of the kind the noise proposed were limited to the five bathrooms, the pantry, and the landing of the back stairs. In fact, one thing more: no one around here locks his house. An intruder has simply to wait until things get quiet and then use a door. Burglary whirls around us in the urban counties, but here the occasional worst offense is the theft of a power tool from the Farmers' Co-op. So I dismissed the idea of a thief. The probable alternative was a raccoon or possum which had clawed its way through screening under the vague impression that opulent garbage lay just within.

I couldn't sleep and I was restless, but I loathed the thought of getting out of bed and doing something constructive. I'd almost persuaded myself that the noise had come from outdoors, a trick of acoustics, when I heard it again, much louder, reaching me not only through the floor but by way of the open stairwell just outside our room.

I've heard that noise so often since, the slight scratch,

the shuffle, the curious suggestion of wood sighing against wood, the *swaying* sound . . . I can separate out the parts now, tell almost exactly when a foot is pushing across the floor, when a claw digs for balance into a crack between boards, when the thing ponderously revolves in the dark to launch another foot forward. I long for the innocence of that first night—the almost-innocence (for had it, after all, shifted slightly that time I caught it unawares?)—when I went downstairs buck naked, flicking light switches ahead of me so that the dark glittered everywhere on windows. At the entrance to the living room I came briefly to a stop. Some years ago my father had had the ugly old ceiling fixture removed, but he'd never got as far as replacing it with another or with wiring some of the wall sockets into the master switch. I wasn't afraid, but I was wary of the encounter of bare toes with the sharp yellow teeth of a possum. And now, holding my breath, I heard the sound again. Since my eyes were not yet adjusted to the dark, I saw nothing. But the sound had seemed to come from some distance away, and carefully I stepped forward from the lighted hallway. The great room stretched before me. All of the glass panels in the terrace wall were open; a faint breeze touched my body and I smelled the slight, delicate fragrance of the spring night. I put on a lamp, and then several more, and began methodically to check under chairs and tables, behind the two sofas, for a small intruder. I lighted my way down the room until it blazed as if it were a beacon on a dangerous coast, and I found nothing. The oiled wood of the furniture glittered, and the floor which Sarah had waxed just that day shone like still water. The terrace screens were firmly latched. None of the mesh was broken.

It was as I turned back from checking the screens that I saw, in the floor near my feet, three semicircular tracks of shallow scratches. They disappeared ahead of me, but they led back to the pedestal, and were most apparent just at its base. They were streaks of light in the black shimmer of the wood. I knelt and rubbed at one, but I couldn't quite take it out. I crawled forward, and felt the track deepen under my finger, as if the hardest part had been getting the pedestal started.

*Someone had moved it, and then moved it back again.* The scratches stopped before each of the three clawed feet. The great, heavy thing had been swung forward and half-round, then forward again onto another foot—that was the only way I could account for the curious shape of the tracks.

But why? and by whom? Suddenly, I felt my nakedness. The room was empty now; I could swear it was empty. But that meant merely that whoever had been here, whoever had played this stupid game in the early hours of the morning, was somewhere else in the house. There was absolutely no point in moving the pedestal: it was set far enough from the wall of glass so that one could walk comfortably behind it. It did not cover a trap door or an ingenious safe or even the bloodstain of a murdered guest. Some sort of joke . . . We knew no one, I would have said, whose sense of humor ran quite on these lines. There was, of course, comedy about our haunted house and haunted hill, but this was the inevitable result of the house's turreted, many-porched architecture and its comparative vastness. And the subject of our possible ghosts hadn't come up in some time, so that the joke—if it was a joke—was ill-prepared for, a punch line for a gag that the audience has forgot about.

Which, rather oddly (given how little I knew then), made me feel all the more uneasy. From where I squatted, at the base of the great pedestal, I looked up its blood-brown flank to the ornate collar that had struck me before as the ruff for a head now severed. Just then something brushed against my buttock and spine, something cold and cloth, a grave dress. I felt my bones dissolve with fear, and swung weakly on the ball of one foot, and my elevated gaze passed from the headless pedestal to the hard, cold face of my wife.

# 9

ELEANOR AND I had become very fond of Ray and Alma Gravatt, though personally I questioned Ray's conscience, his moral courage, and the logical content of his usual sermon from the pulpit of St. Peter's-in-the-Valley. Statistically, he'd done a tremendous job there, turning a limping parish that was about to close down into a booming business with a new building that lacks only a few last refinements. (Of course, it's been a help to Ray that during his years here the area has been planted over with summer homes and motels stuffed with well-heeled tourists anxious to be once-a-year Anglicans.) I didn't discount the deep desire he seemed to have to be truly *good*, and in a way I found his backslipping, his spitefulness, his selfishness and vanity rather endearing. Like many other clerics, he started with a notion of entering the theatre; in the case of the majority of these men, their first thought was the best one, and the most that can be said for their taking orders is that they, probably, have been saved, although perhaps at the expense of numerous congregations. Ray had all the right background for his St. Peter's job: an undergraduate degree from Amherst and, after a few months at Yale's drama school, a B.D. from the Episcopal Theological School. He was a St. Paul's boy —the right St. Paul's—and he'd been married at St. Bartholomew's to a girl who'd gone to Foxcroft and Wellesley and then done the beautifully droll thing of getting an M.A. from Wayne State. But fate took her sense of humor to task by leading her to Ray, whose second job out of seminary was as assistant minister at an in-city church in Detroit. Alma is beautiful, intelligent, warm: to feel her eyes run over you is to curse the commitment she's had to make so fully. And Ray is a narcissist and therefore a man of such limited sympathy that one wonders how he got past the most permissive psychiatrist in his prepostulant tests.

They came, the two of them, the next afternoon for drinks. I am on the vestry, and our ostensible reason for meeting was to discuss ways and means of raising more money for Hilltop Mission. But in fact this was merely another excuse for one of our weekly binges, and Eleanor, who especially liked Ray, had hauled enough liquor and ice and charged water down to the pool to keep a fairly big party going. They found us there around four-thirty, already slightly stoned from a couple of drinks, the heat, our disturbed night, and our several quarrels of the day. These last, of course, had centered on what I was, or seemed to be, doing at the foot of the pedestal. I'd looked "utterly mad," said Eleanor (forgetting the doctors' cautions). Crouching there stark-naked in that blazing room, I'd tried to explain to her, and she'd frowned and become "reasonable" and insisted that Sarah herself must have made the scratch marks—having, perhaps, discovered she'd waxed everywhere except under the pedestal, and then had to move it sideways far enough to finish the job. And the noises I'd heard? How many odd noises *hadn't* we heard since moving to this horrible place? So all right, all right, I'd said finally. I was worshiping a phallic symbol, and she ought to be damn' glad to catch me at it, considering the service I gave her. Which made her sore, and made me groan at the whole mess.

Anyway, enter the Gravatts, also in bathing suits. Since parish life has made them nothing if not quick at diagnosing situations, they at once began a soothing babble designed to put themselves at ease, even if it didn't do much for anyone else. That is the first law of survival in the ministry, I think—and, of course, it usually brings everyone else around soon or late. They'd been to a party at the Hinmans' that had been a real bash; it looked like a sure thing that Mrs. Kemp would give the windows in the west transept (tinted glass right now). The seminarian who drove over from Bexley Hall to take services at Hilltop reported there'd been three new people last Sunday. More, much more, of same, and some local gossip.

Then, at last, the comfortable but (all the same) expectant pause: they'd done the kind of professional job on us that we'd watched them do so often on others. Its secondary aim was to provide the atmosphere in which bad feelings could be aired without embarrassment or further rancor. And to my astonishment Eleanor tumbled straight into the trap. Rolling over onto her back, she held out her glass to me and said, "Get me another one, Johnny—lots of ice." And then, as I went to the bar, she said to Alma and Ray, "I'm absolutely furious with him." But she contrived to sound amused—with me, I suppose, but perhaps with herself also. "You two arrived just in time to head off a divorce."

When she talks about "divorce" this way I know that everything has really been forgiven—if (again) not for one moment forgot. For our childlessness, my illness, our common feeling of expensive but unsatisfactory drifting have made her at times talk seriously of leaving me. Though we share so many enthusiasms, interests, points of view . . . Would it be better for both of us? Was it possible for us to part lovingly? Was it finally going to be the only solution? Solution to what? I sometimes wondered, though seldom aloud. For Eleanor, like Ray, placed her simple faith in generalizations, in phrases with a muted resonance and a little dust across their fine old surface.

Eleanor was in full cry when I came back with her drink—and my night's adventure had become just that. She was now quite prepared to entertain seriously the possibility of an intruder, though she insisted that the likelihood was that Sarah had moved the pedestal herself. Or . . . perhaps the pedestal was haunted? Here, Ray and Alma chimed in brightly, agreeing that the pedestal had a look about it that they didn't quite like. Was it, maybe, *too* big? And was there something . . . well, obscene about those little claw feet? Maybe it was up to all sorts of things once we went to bed, nipping around the house, outdoors even, sending some kind of signal for a coven. We might wake one night and come downstairs and find the living room full of ghostly pedestals met in diabolic rite. Oh, marvelous, marvelous!

By now Eleanor had quite exorcised whatever emotion the sight of me had roused in her (looking into her face as I knelt on the floor, I hadn't known whether to call it hatred, fear, loathing, or some mixture of all three). "I wish you could have seen him," she said, gasping for breath. "Not a stitch—and rubbing one finger on the floor. And that enormous pedestal looming over him."

"I wish I had," Alma replied—and our eyes met. No, Ray would never catch that remark, and Eleanor, it seemed, was too far gone in laughter. I wish you had, too, I thought, and thought she understood. How far is it possible, even generous, to go with the wife of a friend? This wasn't the first time I'd felt that both Alma and I needed a sustenance that neither of our partners provided.

# 10

SARAH ARRIVED next morning with news of a local murder. A woman back in the hills had been found in her derelict farmhouse, her head almost blasted off by a shotgun, and her five children huddling in dumb terror in another room. The children were by various fathers—including, it was said, two of her brothers—and the presumed killer was the man who had last been involved with her, although the nearest neighbors gave it as their impression that he'd not been seen for a week or more, and the children, in so far as any coherent statement could be got from them, suggested he'd been gone even longer. The victim, a nominal Mrs. Kinkus, had worked briefly at the restaurant in Oldchurch, and so was known to rather more people than the average hill dweller is. Eleanor was quite sure she'd talked with her once or twice, and Sarah said that the poor girl—she was only twenty-one—had been at school with her middle daughter. My suspicion was that in fact they were related: in this county that was until recently closed away almost altogether from the urban centers surrounding it, family relationships are so extensive and complicated that it is a dangerous thing to offer the most casual criticism of one local to another. They are usually first, second, or third cousins, once, twice, or three times removed. Sarah said darkly that this kind of thing ran "in their strain"—by which I took it she meant promiscuity and incest, not violent death.

The news of the killing had made Sarah's day—and that of a good many other people, I suspect—and Eleanor too, after a moment of shocked and considering silence, asked the usual questions: who found her? how long had she been dead? if the last man didn't do it, who did? who was looking after the children? But their conversation left me depressed and rather uneasy. It was as if, away in the hills to the south and east of us, a great gong had rung out, the first victim had fallen, and now the reverberations of passion and retribution were spreading across the countryside. The morning was hot and humid—this was, in fact, the hottest spring I ever remembered. Our pines were brown from lack of rain, only their new green candles burning bright, and daily there were grass fires and the shrill of sirens like lightning streaking the heavy stillness. The sky seemed always to be thinly overcast, so that the sun burned down malevolently, a glaring dim. I abandoned my intention of asking Sarah whether she'd moved the pedestal, and I rather doubted that Eleanor would ever remember the question now. Sarah's answer scarcely mattered from my point of view, anyway. Whether she said yes or no, I was left with the quite distinct noises that had got me out of bed and down that flight of steps. Someone had pushed the pedestal that night . . . or, someone had collided in the dark with another piece—several pieces—of furniture. Someone had been in the house. Of course, I thought again of the crime, that wretched girl with her head shot half off, and it was her ghost I put in our house that night—the same night, according to preliminary investigation. She had found her way straight to us.

I wandered outdoors, down the steps, and toward the pine grove along our western border. This cool, murmuring, scented place, where one's footfalls are silent on bedded needles, seems full of beneficence. I lay down for a time, closed my eyes, and in the murmurous silence tried to empty my mind of Eleanor's face as it had looked that night, of Alma's body and Ray's trustful indifference, of a girl shot dead and the sound of women talking, of a pedestal that somebody, for God knew what reason, liked to move around. I must have dozed, for I woke hearing, as it seemed, Eleanor say, "No, definitely not an urn. We'll have to settle for the shotgun. . . ."

I went downhill, and presently the grove yielded to hardwoods and the footing got considerably more precipitous. Off to my left were the terraced levels of garden and pool, garages, tennis court. Here were windfalls overgrown with woodbine and poison ivy, great pin oaks rearing up in their beautiful, gnarled complication, wrist-thick wild grapevines swooping from tree to tree, and exquisite, small clumps of spring flowers in glades. Leaves were not fully out, and far below I could see the river, low for this time of year, a band of pale blue with muddy borders. Small birds flew up from the brush, and overhead I heard the awkward flopping of heavier bodies, of larger wings. Chipmunks scuttered now and then across the path, their tails importantly raised, and some miniature furred or bristled creature shot with orange hustled obliviously toward me and vanished into the bole of a tree. Beautiful great green bugs with spots of crimson sat froglike on weeds and took me in. Far, far above a portion of the white hot sky was clearing to blue.

In a world of such splendor, what were bad dreams? What was one man's life? All the beauty endured; ugly thoughts, miseries, resentments, jealousies, even lusts could not change it. Now, what was true about Eleanor and me? Hadn't we some beauty, too? I loved her, even in my rage, even in my boredom, and believed she loved me just as much. Somehow we would make out, as the oaks did here in the sucking clutter that surrounded them. I would soon be well—physically, I felt wonderfully restored already. I would find a job, however little we needed the money, and give Eleanor what she seemed desperately to want: an identity within a recognizable community.

I turned back, and as I emerged from the woods the house appeared far away and above me, its rear elevation giving it the look of something ungainly and unfinished. The kitchen porch looked gimcrack, tenement-tacked-on, and the steps running down to the sloping yard suggested a grudging concession to a safety ordinance. Nearer to where I stood, the living-room terrace jutted out, glaring white and vaguely nautical, something from a circa-1934 Hollywood musical. Could someone have got onto that terrace without using a ladder? But, no, I was confused. No one had entered the house by way of the terrace: the screens were locked. The visitor must have come through the front or back door. And yet . . . how had he got away? For I came down lighted stairs and through a lighted hall, and heard the pedestal move as I stood in the door to the living room. No one could have hidden from me; it was even more inconceivable that anyone could have slipped past me.

In the heat of the afternoon, the lines of the house wavered, blurred slightly. I remembered a science-fiction serial all of us had gone to, week after week, on childhood Saturday afternoons: about a mysterious underground kingdom destroyed at last by a huge machine that melted everything it turned its light on. There had been a delicious moment when the wicked, beautiful queen, in flowing velvet and a tall collar, dissolved on her throne. Was she about to repent? I couldn't remember. But for a time the afternoon of the present hung suspended in my memory with that long-ago movie, and the one vision was no more fiction than the other, and no years came between them. Either was now; either was long ago.

It was in this state that I saw, or believed briefly that I saw, something I shall put down now, though it is the tailpiece to this narrative, if indeed it ever occurs at all, and therefore out of chronological order. But since it is a scene I shall not witness myself—except as it appeared to take place while I stood at the edge of the woods—it seems proper to give it here.

I looked, then, upward toward what was no longer spring but dusty summer: early, late, I could not say. The house slept in morning sunlight. From the roof a hawk fluttered up, ungainly till the air took his wings. In the silence of my Now there were intimations of sound in that later present. A car went by in the road, a train groaned far down the valley. And then a woman screamed. Moments later Sarah burst open the kitchen door and on panic-quick, stumbling feet crossed the porch, descended the steps, and staggered clumsily down the lawn to the edge of the woods, where she disappeared.

Oh, the thing she'd seen! I knew she'd live out her days on it, and on how she'd struggled, bramble-torn and tree-lost and sick from her terror of heights, to the lower road and safety. What a gift was in our giving!—what a kindness we did her, to destroy that vicarious life and move her to the center of a drama.

I closed my eyes, and the future and the past both re-ceded, grew dumb. As that tale of the melting kingdom had carried no moral or other meaning, but had merely pleased with the spectacle of disaster, so the image of Sarah running in summer sunlight now conveyed nothing that was relevant to the life the three of us led. I asked myself why it should have come to me, and the answer I gave at the time was that I was in the peculiarly fuzzy condition that sometimes follows a too-long nap and a bad dream.

I went on up the hill to the house, and in the front hall came upon the ladies happily absorbed in the shampooing of an Oriental runner. Sarah, apparently, had just polished off another local citizen, for the words I heard as the screen door banged behind me were ". . . a sly one—ask anybody and you'll get the same answer."

# 11

"ALMA, OF all people," Eleanor said that evening. "Sarah was telling me about Alma—or, rather, about what people are saying. Really, no one's immune in a place like this. I suppose they're even talking about us."

"What's Alma done?"

"They don't know for sure, but they all agree she's . . ." Eleanor's voice died away and patches of dull pink stood out on her temples. "No. It isn't right to repeat such things. I've already said too much."

"Exactly. Too much to stop there."

"Did you know she's one of the locals?"

"Local" was a word of dismaying force—it could, on occasion, entirely destroy someone's social standing. The term didn't refer to any particular group in our midst—submentals back in the hills, for instance, ingrown and inbred—but instead was used of anyone born or raised in the township specifically but more generally within the county. The locals themselves used it to typify one another and to "bring down" anyone among them who tried to get a leg up. "He's—or she's—a local," they'd tell you, briefly dissociating themselves from the category and giving you to understand that the worst had been pronounced. Usually the response came as a result of one's having met a local who had seemed particularly agreeable and worth knowing better. "He's a local"—meaning, "He's not worth your time; he was out to impress you, but we know him for what he is." I have never lived in a place where outwardly there was such an easygoing democracy and in reality such a complication of the social structure. The locals might entertain us in their homes, or on rare instances permit us to entertain them, but the spirit was always that of un-equals meeting. As long as we observed our prerogatives and wore them with confidence such occasions would be easy and even pleasant. But if we made too much of an effort to win approval, and in doing so cast aside our seeming superiorities, the atmosphere would chill, the con-versation stumble to a halt. All this would seem to sug-gest that the more rank one assumed the more popular one could become. This was far from the case, however: those who made public their sense of status, though it's doubtful that they knew it, were described as "trash." The difference is a tenuous one, and all of us who were aware of it ex-isted in a state of general apprehension. It was, for instance, perfectly proper to ring for the maid to bring fresh ice (the "maid," quite possibly, was someone you'd had in for a drink the week before—indeed, Eleanor and I had some-times been uncertain, at other houses, whether the lady answering the door was hired for the occasion or merely helping out her hostess). It was altogether improper to *an-nounce* that the maid would be in with more ice in a moment. As I write this I think I perceive where part of the difference lies. The "maid" so referred to might turn out to be, conceivably, your guests' sister-in-law or cousin. It cannot be pleasant to have relatives thus referred to. But . . . if, instead, the host or hostess merely rings a bell, and in a minute in comes Cousin Ella with ice—why, nothing's been said, and the only fact to be apprehended is that Ella, bless her heart, has arrived with just what was needed.

This has been a long excursus, and even so a superficial one. It has touched on some of the unacceptable outsiders—the "trash"—but not on those unacceptable locals who were described as "dirt." And perhaps it hasn't sufficiently emphasized the fact that the position of a local—in the local view—was never open to improvement. He might make money, send a son or daughter to college, but he remained as he started out—except that he'd better watch himself or he might abruptly become "dirt." They were dirt who lived back in the hills, without plumbing, and "played" (in the local euphemism) with their own daughters; they were equally dirt who put on airs and engaged with outsiders as equals.

A long excursus—and all by way of trying to suggest why I was so dismayed to hear Alma called a "local" (and my dismay, of course, was a result of the extent to which local views were getting at me or, to be honest, getting at me and affecting Alma).

I said to Eleanor, after a pause far briefer than the foregoing would suggest, "Alma's no more a local than I am. She was born in Richmond."

"If you're going to bite my head off, I *had* better stop."

"No. No. I'm sorry. I'm just so damn' sick of these spooky distinctions——"

"Please. Don't start on that again. I've heard it too often. I don't care at all what these horrible people think of us—

or what they think of themselves, for that matter."

"For someone that indifferent, you spend a lot of time pumping Sarah."

"I have almost nothing else to do," Eleanor answered coldly. "Sarah's like a pimple that won't clear up. You keep squeezing it to see how much more will come out."

"All right, all right." I put down my fork (have I said that we were at dinner?). "Just tell me what's going around about poor Alma. No. Start by telling me why she's a local."

"Because her grandfather taught at Bexley Hall—years ago, 1894 or '95—and married one of the Brainton girls."

My God! The youngest Brainton "girl" was still alive and resident at Oldchurch. She was in her eighties, at least, but she wore bobby sox, saddle shoes, skirts and blouses in primary colors, and enough rouge and lipstick to keep a drugstore solvent. Miss Brainton and her deceased sisters were famous for having entertained young men of quality, locals, and seminarians until extreme age or the tertiary stage of syphilis forced them into retirement. It was horrible to think that that big-mouthed, blond-dyed, senile infant could be Alma's great-aunt. It was partly horrible because Alma, too, had a big, rather slack-lipped, wet mouth, a liking for bright clothes, a bit of touch-up in her light-brown hair.

"That was all a long time ago," I said irritably. "Anyway, she's only part local, even by their standards."

"Oh, no," Eleanor replied. "Remember? You never marry up, you just pull down. As far as they're concerned, she's one of their own."

"It was her *grand*mother! Seventy years ago. More. Her father's people are Tidewater for generations back."

"That's just dirt moved south," Eleanor replied serenely. "I'm not sure which side you're on."

"No side. Dirt's dirt. You can't clean it up in a couple of generations. Small wonder she's slipped."

"So that's it. Alma's 'slipped,' whatever that means. She's seduced somebody in the choir?"

"Nothing's certain. I told you. It's just that they're down on her. They're pretty sure they know . . . something or other."

"*Friends* of ours!"

She flashed at me. "I *said* it shouldn't be repeated."

"You made damn' sure I heard the whole of it." But that was thoroughly unfair. I shook my head to show her I was sorry and said, "No. Of course you didn't. It's just that I'm shocked. The malice, the plain human meanness. *My* family started out in Oak Harbor. Do you suppose they'd crucify me there if I went back?"

"It might depend on what they thought you were up to."

"You don't *believe* this talk about Alma!"

"I have the greatest admiration for Ray. I can't believe that anyone he chose would be other than . . . than top drawer."

"Anyone he *chose!* You sound like a cockeyed Calvinist talking about divine election. Ray is a very sweet, dumb guy with all the sentimentality of an elderly fairy and all the snobbism of the kind of kids we grew up with."

"I'm not sure I know what you're trying to tell me. That Alma was a sweet, dumb mistake?"

"Oh, Christ. I mean that Ray's a nice lovable jerk. The sad thing is that Alma married *him*."

"I wondered if that might be what you were working

round to," said Eleanor thoughtfully. "It may come as a surprise, but I'm perfectly aware of your interest in her. I wonder if it works both ways?"

Part of me was gratified by this show of jealousy, or would be when I had time to think the scene over rationally. The rest of me was boiling mad.

"There hasn't been one thing between us that . . . that even Sarah could take exception to."

"Yet."

"Ever. She's my friend's *wife!*"

Eleanor stood up abruptly, pushing back her plate with a force that nearly set the wine and water glasses reeling. "Is that the reason? Not that I'm *your* wife but that she's *his*."

"Darling! No. My God, no, no! I didn't mean it that way at all. Look." I got up, too. "We're almost done here, and we don't ever have to come back. I'll get a job in New Zealand, Brazil, anywhere a long way away from here. Just . . . let's keep the peace until we go. Honey? That isn't too much, is it? Let's just get along with everybody for the time that's left."

"Whatever made you think I was longing for New Zealand or Brazil?" asked Eleanor coolly. "And don't tell me that slut hasn't got other ideas and you'd love to go right along with them." With that, she left the room.

# 12

I was beginning to get superstitious about parties, for our quarrels now seemed connected with them. Tonight, for instance, we were having a couple dozen people in for drinks, including Alma and Ray. Still, better a party, maybe, than a long evening of angry silence. Eleanor had headed for the kitchen, and assuming she was getting ready to pile things into the dishwasher I collected our plates and cups and saucers and carried them out. It wasn't entirely a conciliatory gesture; I wanted to gauge how mad she was at me. She took the china without comment and started scraping off the plates into the disposal. I went back for the silver and a couple of serving dishes, and then finally for the glasses.

"I suppose I'd better get dressed," I said then.

"I suppose you had."

"Or I can put this stuff in to wash, if you'd rather go ahead. . . ."

"No. I want to get the food ready."

I knew what that meant: she'd fiddle with things we were going to serve later until I'd changed and returned downstairs. No chance for a reconciliation. On the other hand, she'd answered me quite civilly, so matters between us could have been worse.

"I'll carve when I come down."

"Yes. And *thin*. The last time it looked as if we'd shopped at a church supper."

Country parties are simple, but this fresh air really does seem to give people uncommon appetites. The beef roast I was to carve was nearly nine pounds, but sliced thin or paper-thin it would be gone by midnight. So would the big platters of marinated artichoke hearts, the bowls of shrimp, and the huge pâté. Eleanor and Sarah had buttered five loaves of french bread for the beef and pâté, and these too would vanish long before the guests themselves did. I was fairly sure the liquor would hold out, since after a couple of near disasters we'd decided that the only safe estimate was three guests to a bottle.

I went into the living room to check the bar, which I'd set up before dinner, and in the last light coming from the terrace windows I saw the pedestal moving slowly, clumsily back into its place. A shuffle, a scrape, a perilous swing, and it was motionless again.

# 13

Sometimes I have dreamed of my ultimate confrontation of the Enemy, who is still faceless but this time leaves me in no doubt of what's in store for me. And I have heard myself scream, felt my head explode with the years and years of rage and hatred, and then found that my breath was short, I was gasping, I could not talk or move for panic and dismay. The Enemy, approaching no closer, destroyed me where I stood. And, yes, it *was* rather as if he were a great machine melting me away. I died humiliated by my ineffectual rage, my useless hatred. I died ashamed of my cowardice.

I mention this dream because the actual experience was so different. I knew as I watched—really *saw*—the monstrous thing settle back in place that this was indeed the enemy, the killer, and that it had been listening to us tonight, to our quarrel. The time I'd spent carrying dishes to the kitchen was the time it had needed to get back to its original position—not quite time enough, in fact. I knew this, and knew that it followed my thoughts, and that my knowledge barely concerned it. It believed itself secure—

from me, from any of us—in its power. It had waited its time for us, all these years, all the distance between us. And in an old house by a river, at a commonplace auction, it had moved out of its dark, spider-thick corner and finally into our lives. Or perhaps it would be truer to say that it moved finally into the lives of those who were prepared to receive it. We had turned it loose.

I felt as if never before had I possessed such lucidity. There the thing was, beautiful, composed, in the composed, beautiful room—my enemy and perhaps my death. If it was unconcerned to be caught, I, in a somewhat different way, was unconcerned to catch it. I was neither frightened nor infected with a sense of the marvelous. Why shouldn't Evil animate what it chooses—setting tables to rapping, chairs to dancing, pedestals to walking? Was I even surprised? Now, knowing so much of its ways, I can't remember. I think I must have been, though even surprise was probably sunk in the calm and rationality that held me for the time. After all, I had caught it once before, the night I'd put down movement to a trick of moonlight. And another night I'd heard it, and put down *that* to a midnight visitor, though I'd found tracks that supported a very different explanation. You could say that the pedestal, delicately, had prepared me, and also that I was at work preparing myself. For these long, silent days of recuperation had built up in me a suspense, an expectation. Innocently, I had thought of a brilliant flowering of my life, of the apparition of something impossibly wonderful but absolutely right and irrefutably real. It might take the form of a baby, or a love affair; even of a job. Whatever it was, it would redeem Eleanor as well as me. I had felt quite strongly that we would both be involved and transformed.

[ 48 ]

Then the gong had rung out over the hills; murder had been done; and into my mind crept the first uncertainty. Disaster, too, has its brilliant flowering. Far away down the room from me, the pedestal stood up darkly red like a plant with an immense stalk and no bloom as yet. Was it part of the plan that we still had nothing to decorate it with? For how would the thing get around, weighted down with an urn or a candelabrum or a bust? I had a terrible desire to laugh at the absurdity of the image this conjured up, the pedestal tilting, swaying, shuffling across the dark while a merely mortal artifact skidded on its top, lost all solid footing, and crashed to the floor. Hadn't Eleanor suggested putting a shotgun on it? That had plenty of surface, would ride back and forth before it finally went. But, no, of course she hadn't; I'd dreamed that notion and given it to her. If a shotgun came into this, it must be aimed at the pedestal, used to blast it, spoil it.

And to what purpose? I thought—and at that moment began to walk toward it. You can't kill death; you can't destroy Evil as simply as someone had demolished the head of a subliterate girl who was threatening, perhaps, to make a nuisance of herself.

I touched the pedestal on its flank, and it was cold, very cold. How could wood be as cold as this on a hot spring evening? My hand ran down the smooth, silky side, and when I took it away I saw a delicate slick of oil on my skin—Sarah had faithfully carried out her job of "feeding" the finish. But what was feeding the rest of it; or what, in a frightful hunger, was it going to have to devour before too much time went by?

Suddenly I felt that we were fools to have this party, that it would do nothing to save either of us and might expose others to the danger. I had a desperate desire to talk to someone, but Eleanor would outwardly be angry with me, and secretly scornful—or sad and pitying, moved perhaps forever beyond my reach by a sense of hopelessness. The obvious person, of course, was Ray, whose imagination and devotion should have made him responsive to whatever kind of energy, force, the marvelous could command. But Ray was a clergyman as I might have been a television announcer or a brush salesman. Or as he might have been. I remembered an outbreak of alleged poltergeist activity in England a few years back, and how peevish the Church had been with those clerics who made an effort at exorcism. There was the Church for you, sensible, matter-of-fact, calmly suggesting that you try a leap of faith to God and brushing off the minor amazements that might make you think you could survive such a leap. And there was Ray. Good and bad in his world were defined as parish triumphs and grievances. He was the small in the large, and a matter of evil would make him petulant and reproachful.

Then I thought of Alma, who had so much of the divine openness poor Ray was innocent of. But, looking at the pedestal, I wondered whether my brain was working exactly as it was expected to. I even wondered whether I had really "caught" the pedestal getting back to its place, or whether it had hung, balanced on one sharp clawed foot, until it knew I was watching from the doorway. I sensed, at least, that between us there was some momentous conspiracy.

# 14

DURING THE first part of the evening, almost everyone talked about the shooting. It was rumored that somebody "prominent" was involved—whether as killer or witness, or in a more obscure role, no one seemed sure: naturally, people hoped for the worst. It wasn't clear either where the rumor had sprung from, though Eleanor said cynically "I could guess," and flashed a half-smile at Sybil Fruig, one of those with whom we "shared" Sarah. It seemed to me probable that Eleanor's joke really spoke the truth, that one Sarah or another had encountered still another Sarah, and that from speculation and half-known, wholly misunderstood fact these two had each turned away with the substance of the rumor fully agreed on. And God help whatever male had happened to cross their dark view when the suspicions were formulated; as possession by demons is said to afflict the most vulnerable, so this other kind of possession afflicts the random innocent.

I sat down next to Alma, who'd been very quiet since arriving and was still holding her first drink, and said, "Eleanor's right, I imagine, though I wish she wouldn't make fun of someone she spends so much time industriously pumping."

"She meant Sarah, I suppose."

"Yes; but I mean somebody like Sarah. The village, the valley, the whole place is full of them. And rub any two together——"

"Now you're sounding like Eleanor."

"Sorry. It's so easy to be a snob here. I never felt like a snob in my life until I settled in the country."

"You never knew anyone to have that sort of feeling about until you came to the country."

"Oh, didn't I?—kids at school and college, the army, the office . . . And yet you're right, in a way. We're so hot in each other's pockets here, for all the distance between the houses we live in. I was just thinking about Bessie Ludlow. We're never sure when Bessie opens someone's door whether she's maid for the day or guest of honor."

Alma smiled. "Then pity the rector's wife."

"I do. One blooper could mess up the whole parish." But I wasn't, then, thinking really of Alma's problems or the larger one of being a generous person in a community that encouraged every sort of subtle social division. My thoughts were on our shooting, and the sudden appearance in the drama of someone "prominent." I said, expecting Alma to follow me, "I suppose they could mean anyone, or that everybody could mean someone different."

"They?"

"The villain in the case—in the shooting."

Alma shuddered and looked, for a moment, as if she might be ill. I took her drink, warm now, the glass bleary with fingerprints, from a shaking hand. "I'm all right," she said weakly. "Or I will be. Just get me a bit more ice, will you?" When I returned she added, "I've heard too much about it. And the details are . . ." But her voice died. She took a breath and after a brief sip from her glass said, "She was one of our protégées, you know."

"One of St. Peter's? No, I didn't. There's no reason I should have, I suppose. But I see how . . . Did you ever meet her?"

"A few times. And I went out there once with some clothes for all of them. Frankly, I thought she was a lost cause, poor tragic creature. But Ray . . . You know how Ray is. He was the one who kept the humane officer from taking the children. He had a talk with Lenore Davil. She's judge at the juvenile court, in case you don't know. Ray persuaded her to let him see what he could do. You can imagine how he feels now."

I was appalled for Ray, for his distress, for the failure of his conviction; and I was ashamed of the opinion of him I'd had since we first met, of the opinion I'd expressed to myself only a short time before. No one who took so much trouble over a worthless girl, a clutch of helpless, dirty, but sacred small humanity, could be as entirely absorbed in himself, in his own image, as I had supposed.

"I'm dreadfully sorry," I said, "but I admire Ray for keeping faith in her. And, who knows?—if somebody hadn't . . . If she'd lived, maybe . . ."

"Yes," said Alma wearily. "Well, it will all work out somehow. Sometime or other. Go on with what you were saying."

I didn't, immediately, remember. "About the prominent person in the case, do you mean? I was wondering whether 'prominent' to—say—Bessie Ludlow would be 'prominent' to you or me. Was this person a prominent storekeeper or somebody on the village council or the manager of the lodge or one of us?"

" 'Prominent,' " Alma replied, "always means"—she spoke, as it seemed, with great pain—"one of us."

"One of us what?" asked Sybil Fruig, coming up. She looked so bright-eyed that I felt sure she was one of those three-to-a-bottle people we'd had to learn to plan for.

"One of us did the shooting," I answered. Perhaps because I'd had a few drinks myself, it was a moment before I noticed that Alma had risen and left us and was almost to the hallway door.

Sybil let out the terrible, paralyzing scream that indicates she's been moved by the sense of humor everyone tells her is "delicious." Her husband, Bob, who knows all her signs of danger, materialized immediately and took her by an arm. "What's the big joke?" he asked.

Sybil clung to him and screamed again, her face drooping toward his shoulder. "One of us did the murder," she said. "That's what Johnny says. Somebody right here in this room."

# 15

I'D SAID nothing of the sort, or quite of the sort, anyway, and I was dismayed at the silence that fell around us. I had again the sense of observing the set for a movie, although now the music had all gone. Briefly, everyone was motionless, and the pose of each struck me as manic, gleeful in a tense, murderous way. I could have believed any one of them, male or female, a killer who had lately held a shotgun. It was quite terrible, and for the time it lasted inescapable. My eyes went to the pedestal, looming beyond women's bare shoulders, the wilted shirts of men. It seemed entirely possible that it communed with the killer, and that the killer therefore was one of these people, someone we called a friend.

"I said . . ." I began feebly, but already the talk had started up again; someone laughed; someone accused Bob Fruig of the crime. The witticism bent Sybil nearly double. The talk grew wilder, more tasteless, as it will when people discuss a disaster that seems to have no bearing whatever on their own lives and can't even be imaginatively entered into. It was unthinkable that anyone here would ever shoot anyone else—anyone not of their own sort, at least.

Except . . .

It occurred to me that Alma might know a good deal more than she had any right to reveal. The wife of a rector must often find herself possessed of facts that, like a meteor- ologist watching a radarscope, she can see gathering into storm long before the winds rise locally and the rain be- gins. She had been so quiet, subdued . . . and the dead woman had been one of St. Peter's cases. I looked round for Ray and didn't see him, but I caught Eleanor's eye (baleful) and decided she was angry with me because of Sybil's outburst. I got up, meaning only to move a little farther from Eleanor's presence, but like a snake she wrig- gled through the mob and struck at me as I turned toward the hallway door.

"She's on the porch." I must have looked an honest puzzlement, for she added, "Sweet little quiet little Alma."

"Oh? I guess she's . . . upset."

"I'm upset, too, if that matters at all. It would help if you'd get these barflies out of here and into the dining room. The food's just . . . *sitting*."

"It's early yet. They always find it sooner or later. You ought to know *that*, at least."

"I know plenty more," she said in a tight, shaking voice. "I could tell you things about some of your dear friends that would send you right back off the deep end. And maybe I will," she added. "Maybe I will, one day quite soon."

And then she turned away from me, so coldly, so angrily that I was stricken; I felt death touch my hand. I had been ill; I knew I had been difficult. Had I pressed her so hard that now there was no action of mine in which she didn't find a sign of danger, no intention that didn't yield multiple interpretations, all bad?

I set about the job of herding people into the dining room; I became the professional host. And those who'd found their way to the food I chivvied back to the bar for fresh drinks. Alma didn't return, and I couldn't find Ray. I felt ill, fragile; Eleanor's words had once again destroyed my whole sense that, whatever our differences, we loved and trusted one another. I wished everyone would go home; I wished passionately that I too had a home to go to, someone to care for me, someone who wouldn't scold, or scorn, or make fun, or briskly ignore. Absurdly, I even wished I had a dog that I could go out in the woods with, later, and sit in the dark and feel beside me, and know that it loved me and held no grudges, no hard, unforgiving memories.

So it was that when, a little later, I came on Alma in a high-backed chair in the room we use for television, I didn't say to her any of the things I might have said, or tried to say, earlier. It was peaceful just to sit next to her, even though I knew that much of her toleration of me was due to her ignorance of how sick and crazy I'd been a while back. I didn't care what she might know of the shooting. I wanted balm; I wanted friendship, kindness. I was glad to be one of two bodies at tired rest.

I said finally, "It isn't hot punch we're serving tonight. Do you want some more ice in there, at least?" For she still carried with her the same smeared, half-finished glass of whiskey.

"Why does Eleanor dislike me so much?—and all of a sudden, it seems."

I might have tried for a diplomatic response, but when

[ 57 ]

Eleanor's hostility is aroused it can never be interpreted as anything else, and diplomacy is wasted effort. Besides, I thought too much of Alma to dissimulate to her. Instead, I made a stab at explaining what seemed to me the real difficulty—which wasn't Alma at all.

"Eleanor's depressed about me," I said. "I'm not . . . responding, she thinks."

"And is that the case?"

"I don't know. Everything was fairly okay until we bought"—I could hear my voice wavering with embarrassment—"that damned pedestal."

"Oh," said Alma thoughtfully.

Her courtesy made me smile. "Yes. 'Oh.' She thinks I've got . . . some kind of fixation."

"Have you?"

"I have now, certainly. In fact, I think I want to talk to Ray about it. I've definitely——" But I couldn't bring it out, not even to Alma in that moment of closeness; I couldn't say, I've definitely seen it moving. I shook my head. "Never mind. You'd lose your last faith in me, too. Anyway, the pedestal's made trouble between us, stupid as that sounds. And this shooting . . ."

"Yes, it was terrible, terrible. We've all been shocked." She spoke hurriedly, as if to brush off the killing or to reduce it to a commonplace. I wondered once again how much more she knew than she could tell.

"I don't want to harp on it," I said. "I'm sure it's painful for you, and worse for Ray. But the thing is that the dead girl's got into it, too, you see."

"Into . . . ?"

I threw out my hands. "Into the pedestal, into me, Eleanor. . . . That killing: I thought the other day it was

[ 58 ]

like a gong ringing out over the whole countryside. It was announcing the doom of all of us."

"Oh, please . . ." Alma stood up, rubbing her hands together, the drink forgotten on the table beside her chair. Her face was creased with distress, empty of color.

I leaned forward and took her hands between mine and drew her toward me. "I'm sorry—whatever I said. I'm so sorry. I only wanted you to know that Eleanor's . . . upset these days. She doesn't really dislike anybody, but she has to strike out, hit at whoever's handy." I got awkwardly to my feet and moved one hand, gently, to her shoulder. She drooped below me, her belly endearingly pushed out against the silky fabric of her dress. I could see straps where her neckline had slipped sideways, and tiny freckles on her back. A drop of saliva crooked down her chin.

She pulled away, crossed the room to a window, and after a moment said, "Perhaps we ought to keep apart for a time."

I hate such proposals because they make human actions and emotions, which ought to be fluid, spontaneous to the moment and the event, as inflexible as the rule-makings of amateur committees. More, if the four of us didn't go on seeing one another there would be talk, and inevitably it would involve either Ray and Eleanor or Alma and me. With the gossip which, if Sarah was any barometer, was going on about Alma and her background, the chances were that she and I would be the subjects of speculation. I wouldn't have brought such an embarrassment on her at any time, let alone now when she seemed so acutely distressed about a matter of far more concrete existence, but weakly I said, "It's up to you. Whatever you decide."

"Oh, yes!" she answered with astonishing bitterness. "Up to me again. Always up to me. Well." She turned round and faced me, bracing herself against the sill. "I've already said it, haven't I? Good-by for a while, Johnny. Good-by."

# 16

THE PARTY went on, it seemed, for hours, but I'd lost all pleasure in it. I carted around a highball, as smeared of glass and as iceless as Alma's, merely to strike the note of the convivial host. The food disappeared and finally the liquor began to run low, but still no one made even perfunctory movements toward leaving. I kept a periodic lookout for Ray; if this was our final meeting, I wanted urgently to talk with him. Temporarily I'd put aside my reservations; I felt that I badly needed counsel. But whenever I saw him he was deep in a circle, and I was too tired and despondent to think up an ingenuity sufficient to extricate him and get him to myself somewhere. Then, by chance, I opened a door on him taking a leak when I'd come upstairs with the same idea, and I asked him to wait and then led him along to the room my grandmother used to have, which is as sheeted and shuttered as it was when she last left here. I thought it was one place we would be safe from company.

He was awfully drunk, and furious with Sybil Fruig. She had said something unforgivable to him, although he refused to go into details. He talked about putting it right between the bitch's legs and seeing what she had to say *then*—which was very unlike him. I wondered whether Sybil had made a crack about his capabilities—though, again, this was most unlike her. Her indiscretions are usually more imaginative and less personal. I suddenly remembered the talk that was, or probably was, going around about Alma, but raping another man's wife didn't seem to me a particularly sensible response to a scandal about your own wife, and Ray is sensible even in his cups. Or, rather, he has a strong sense of self-preservation.

I decided to change the subject, if I could, and said, "I'm sorry about that girl, Ray—the girl who was murdered. Alma told me about your connection with her." His face, which had been an ugly red, went white, and one hand fluttered up in what seemed to be protest. I was dismayed to think I'd added to his distress and went on hurriedly: "I'm sure no one blames you. You'd never have sponsored her if she hadn't seemed to have a chance. It didn't work out, and that's terrible, but it might have—and your job's the long shot, isn't it?"

He turned his face away from me; I felt he couldn't bear even my sympathy. "The long shot," he muttered. But his color began to return and his breathing became more normal. "Alma told you——?"

"Nothing she shouldn't have," I assured him. "Just that you'd interceded for the family, asked that the girl be given another chance. Alma wouldn't ever say too much, you know, even to me—us."

"Alma's discretion," he muttered, "is notorious."

The remark was double-edged—intentionally so, I suspected; and as a friend I didn't feel I could pass it over. "I understand there's been talk . . . ." I began.

Once again that look of terror clamped down on his features. "Has there?" His voice expired on the last word.

"Nobody in the parish is going to believe it, though they may listen for their own amusement."

"Amusement!" he managed to say wonderingly.

"Well, you know: the rector's wife . . . I don't remember any stock jokes on the subject, but there must be some. And Alma is a prize victim: beautiful, kind, responsible. When people have a chance to get their licks in at someone like that, I suppose the impulse is almost irresistible."

He was silent for a time; he seemed to be fumbling for a response. "So that's come out, has it?" he said finally.

"Why, yes," I answered, surprised. "I thought you . . . I thought that was what you meant."

"Forget it," he said harshly, and shifted in his chair. "I'll take care of Alma. What's *your* problem?"

I was put off now not so much by his drunkenness as by a kind of brutality in his features, in the lines of his body, in the way he crossed one thigh over the other, so that the thick, tough muscles showed through the thin cloth. There was a long white scar on that thigh where no black, curly hair grew. He'd got it, he said, in his second year at seminary, in a fight with an Italian sailor at a bar in Scollay Square. I remembered Alma telling us that until recently he'd shaved his legs in summer because he wanted to minimize the pale, shirred line. I'd always assumed he was in that shabby bar on some kind of mission work, but suddenly I questioned that assumption. I questioned my whole mental portrait of him. I didn't know what else he was, what more or other, but I felt uneasy, uncertain of how to go on. I'd been prepared to deal with a fairy-friend, an aging Narcissus, a petulant child. But this brutal, cruel-mouthed man: whatever his reaction, I shouldn't know how to guide myself by it.

Nevertheless, I said, "You know pretty much everything about my trouble, don't you?"

Magically, rather frighteningly, his features shrank, composed themselves into their customary expression of suffering patience. "I know what you've told me—and Eleanor. And what your rector wrote me when you came down here."

"You know then that I've never . . . that delusions weren't one of my problems."

He looked at me with what was either amusement or contempt. "Your biggest problem, boy, is that you've never had one."

"That's true for Eleanor, too," I answered, stung.

"Oh, no! Oh, no! She's got *you.*"

Before this evening, I'd have said to him, "I wish I knew which side you're on"—but that's the sort of remark you make to someone whose sympathy you trust in, and quite suddenly I knew that I had lost him or had never had him at all. The sides were forming: Eleanor and Ray against me; and Alma and I . . . But what side were we on, and for what purpose? I might have felt more indignant with Ray, or more pleasurably forlorn at his desertion, if I in my turn hadn't always had reservations where he was concerned. Nevertheless, I'd always liked him, hadn't I? Didn't I? Or didn't it matter, since we wouldn't be seeing much of one another for a while; from now on?

I hauled myself off the mattress where I'd been sitting, straightened the dust cover, and said, "I guess you're right. Eleanor's got me. Well . . ." I was groping for something that would bring our talk easily, naturally, to an end. We were too far from each other to make a confidence possible.

He reached toward me with a hand and lightly touched my jacket. "Don't be so damn' prickly," he said, rather in his usual manner. "If you can't face facts you *are* sick."

"Has Eleanor been complaining about me?"

"Of course she has. I'm her priest, remember? Can you think of a better person?"

As to that, yes, I could. Ray was inexcusably newsy about his parishioners' problems. One might as well expect reticence in Sarah. Absurdly, the fact of his cloth made those who went to him in trouble rationalize their concern about his indiscretion: he never passed on anything "bad" or "serious," or at least he only told his friends! It took a good forty-eight hours for the news to get around the county.

When I had decided to talk to him about the pedestal, it wasn't with any expectation that he'd keep quiet. The story was too prime; maybe the best he'd ever had handed to him. But because I'd finally come to feel that he was a better priest than I'd ever believed him to be, I thought he might help me in whatever way he could. And if he carried the tale of a haunted pedestal from one household to another . . . well, how much publicity can Evil stand? How much laughter? The effect might be that of opening a musty, dirty room to air and sunlight. Eleanor would be furious, and embarrassed at the talk and laughter. But she could scarcely condemn me for Ray's compulsive news-mongering.

"Okay," said Ray, into my silence. "Tell me about this delusion of yours that you never have."

Against my will, I laughed. Drunk, angry, hostile, he

was still a professional; he never mislaid his bag of tricks. The question was so disarming that I found it almost impossible not to yield to it.

"Something you already know about," I told him. "The pedestal."

"Pedestal?" He grinned. "That thing downstairs you got at the auction?"

I nodded. "I think it's going to do something terrible."

He looked blank. "Terrible," he said at last. "Pedestal. I should have known you wouldn't be suffering from any of the usual fantasies. What's the matter—is it out to get you if you don't put something on top of it soon?"

"A decoration's the last thing it wants. That would hamper its style." Before I had time for second thoughts I said quickly, "It moves."

He didn't show any surprise; composure, after all, is his stock in trade. But I wondered whether he was making a quick note of the curtains and dust covers in the room, in case I got violent and had to be lashed to a bedpost. "You mean that it gets around physically?"

"I mean exactly that. I caught it tonight. I'm not sure— I almost think it meant me to catch it. Before now I've thought . . . naturally, I've thought of more reasonable explanations."

"Explanations for what?"

I told him about the noises on the night before he and Alma came for drinks. Then I went on to describe my encounter with it just prior to the party. Then, belatedly, I told him about the time when, as I now felt sure, I'd seen it shift slightly while it was lying on its side.

"It's got so much bolder," I wound up, "since——" Then

I remembered Ray's defense of the dead girl, and broke off. We'd said enough on the subject, and what connection, after all, could there be between a death in the hills and a pedestal from an old house far away?

"Since when?" he asked.

"Since that girl was shot," I answered reluctantly. "It's as if her killing had . . . unleashed the thing. No. That isn't quite what I feel. It's as if her dying had let loose all the evil around us, all kinds of things that might never have got free if she hadn't . . . if that hadn't happened to her. The pedestal's just part of what's going on."

I thought of the stories that were circulating about Alma; about Eleanor's jealousy and the resulting disintegration of our friendship with the Gravatts; about the pronounced, and not attractive, change in Ray that I had first noticed only minutes earlier; about the equivocal position in which his well-meant interference on the murdered girl's behalf would place him with local authorities.

Ray made no reply. He seemed so far away from me that I added, partly from long-withheld irritation and partly from genuine concern, "You never talk about evil. If it isn't a mental failing it's a social deprivation that's at fault. Sometimes I wonder whether the only hell you can envision is the Church's next General Convention."

That got a perfunctory smile. "You'll have to give me a little time," he said. "If you mean that I've never been seized with the desire to give a sermon on pedestals, or to consult with my bishop about them, you're right. You're positive you've seen it move?"

"As positive as I am you're talking to me now."

"But the rest . . . It hasn't *done* anything, has it?"

"Is it going to have to *do* something before you——"

He got heavily to his feet and then stood propped against the back of the chair, shaking his head as if to clear it. "Take it easy. I know you're worried. This is just a bit much for me to cope with right now."

Whether "now" referred to the fact that he was still upset because of the shooting or more simply that he was too drunk to think coherently, I wasn't sure. Both, perhaps.

"You don't seem very surprised," I said.

"About your pedestal?"

I nodded. I had expected a challenge, or an attempt at rationalization. I had felt sure I'd see a light come into his eyes as this newsworthy item was conveyed to him. "Has there been a rash of cases?"

"No. No rash. We're in short supply on pedestals hereabouts. I suppose the thing is that I've conditioned myself to the miraculous."

"I'd have thought that was the last kind of conditioning any churchman needed."

"Would you?" he said indifferently. He stifled a yawn and then looked quite openly at his wristwatch. "You lead a sheltered life, here on your hilltop. I suppose you might very well think that." He took a couple of uncertain steps toward the door, then straightened himself and went on with an attempt at briskness. "Let's talk tomorrow, Johnny. I'll drop around after lunch, if that's all right for you. But I think right now I'd better collect Alma and get her home."

Alma, however, had left, after a flaming argument with Eleanor which had broken up the party. Ray and I descended to a house that was empty except, ironically enough, for Sybil and her husband, who said merely that Alma had taken the Gravatt car and asked them to wait

[ 68 ]

and bring Ray. I suppose Ray assumed, as I did, that their solemn manner was a drunken attempt to ape sobriety. There was no sign of Eleanor.

Needless to say, probably, I did not have the promised talk with Ray on the next afternoon.

# 17

I woke the following morning with a splitting headache, and for once liquor wasn't the cause. By the clock the time was a few minutes after ten; since the clock ran fast, I guessed it was closer to nine-thirty. Eleanor, though, was already gone—a small mercy for which I was, just then, deeply thankful. I turned on my back and lay spread-eagled under the sheet while the morning tumescence gradually abated. I marveled at the body's blind vitality, which no aggravation of the brain's life seems able to deter. We hadn't made love in so many days that I was vividly aware of the weight of the sheet and hesitant to move a second time until sensation was past. I wondered, grimly, if we would ever make love again. It seemed impossible that we shouldn't, and yet what had happened between us when the party was over had pretty well destroyed what was left of our marriage.

I'd found her—long after seeing off Ray and the Fruigs—sitting on that rickety flight of back steps. The time was well into morning and, baffled and mildly irritated, I'd hunted the house through before looking outdoors. I'd supposed, in my ignorance, that she'd got tighter than usual and holed up somewhere to throw it up or sleep it off. She was immaculate as the fussiest cat, and got to work on herself the moment disorder threatened. She hated even me to see her under anything less than the appropriate control.

So. I found her at last, on the steps, and as the kitchen door swung wide and light fell down them she backed away from me, her eyes brightly yellow in the glow, her skin empty of color, her mouth a little black ugly hole.

"Well, finally," I said. "It's nearly three. Let's hit the sack. You must have enough fresh air to last the rest of the month."

"Enough of everything," she said in a peculiar, gasping voice. "Everything. And you—my God, I've had my fill of you!"

I was too tired, and far too sober, to enjoy the kind of rhetoric she indulges in sometimes in order to summon up drama. Besides, I'd decided in my innocence that the party had been a fairly good one, and I wanted to go to bed in that state of virtue one feels when dull tasks have produced a pleasant ending. I even felt an added virtue: I'd made no pass at Alma when a pass might have succeeded, and without arrogance or contempt I'd set my problem before Ray. Given the man I was, these were excellent accomplishments. I thought I deserved better than fresh dilemma.

"Honey, I'm bushed," I said placatingly. "And you must be, too—you did most of the work. Let's just get some sleep. Do you feel all right now?"

To my astonishment and dismay, she turned farther away from me, went down several steps, and with her head lowered, so I saw only the curly back ends of her hair, said,

"No. I'm not all right. I can't ever be all right. I couldn't be all right unless you'd never been born."

I started toward her. "Look . . . look . . ." I said. "Darling!"

She began to cry. "Or if you were dead. That would be as good as anything could be. How much I wish you'd die!" The words came out muffled by the two fists pushed against her face, and for a long, incredulous moment I tried to fit another speech to her mouth. Then I began to shake, with fright first (it is terrible to believe yourself so much hated), then from the certainty that I was going to be physically sick, and finally from a rage that exploded in my head and left me for the time both sightless and deaf to normal sound. Amid the clamor and the searing lights in my brain I took another step; if my hands had found her body I would probably have sent her down the rest of that flight and then finished her with a rock.

Instead, I stumbled and fell heavily on a knee that in some way had got crossed under my other leg, so that it took my full weight. I suppose I'd lost all coordination. The pain was so agonizing that I was restored to the moment and yet made temporarily indifferent to our argument by sheer animal misery. I got somehow into a seated position and began to massage myself. I wondered if I were going to faint.

Eleanor turned back toward me; curiously, as if my accident hadn't happened, or was faked. "Go ahead and whimper!" she said. "And go ahead with your girl friend, too. I couldn't care less. I told her tonight exactly what she was. I told her . . ." Her voice had become steadily louder, had got high, keening. Now she rushed up past me; I couldn't make out the words she threw back.

"Told her what? What?" I shouted, and sidled round to where I could grasp a rail and pull myself erect. On one leg, hopping, I drew myself after her.

Despite my pain and confusion, I was aware of how Eleanor halted just above me, how she turned, and in what a contemptuous voice she said, "Oh, you fish! You poor stupid fish. I told her she was finished here. I told her she could sleep with every dirty farmer in the county, but she'd never get in *my* house again!"

I was appalled. I watched her face reflect the ugly fury of her mind, and I truly thought I would faint, that I couldn't bear one more moment of this hideous scene. Instead, and to my shame, I began to cry. To hide my face I lowered it on my hands, clenched around the rail. I had nothing to say to her, and I didn't want her to watch my grief. What I wept for, or how much I wept for, I'm still not sure: Eleanor's hatred and the sorrow that surely she would feel a little later on, my own sorrow, our lives together—that common experience we'd wanted to love and enrich; my tears were for all of these things, and for our two lonelinesses and for the joy it had seemed once we had had in each other. I cried to see my life go clean to smash.

"Go ahead and bawl," Eleanor said above my head—a horrible benediction. "*I've* no tears." I looked up at her, and incredibly she laughed, a laugh that shook her body so that she reached for the back door handle in order to steady herself. "God damn you both," she said, and then the laughter seized her again. She pulled open the door and stumbled through it, but when it had closed she pushed her forehead against the screening and stared out at me as if my grief were a thing too precious to abandon. In the light from the kitchen fixture I could see that her mouth and chin were wet with slobber. "You and that sainted whore. God damn both of you straight to the coldest hell."

I pulled myself up the remaining steps as rapidly as I could, but my wrists were so weak, my hands shook so much, that it was a long process. Then, half hobbling, half hopping, I crossed the porch and went inside. She was at the sink, ostensibly scraping a platter. Her face was dry and she appeared immaculate and composed. But as I approached she put the platter down, looked at the plate- and glass-cluttered counters, and with a shrug started toward the front of the house. "Anyway," she observed, "Sarah's coming in again tomorrow. She's giving us an extra day."

No remark, at that particular time, could have immobilized me more effectively. It was so much a part of the old life between us that I felt horror, even something like fear, as I watched her. At the door to the butler's pantry, which connects the kitchen and the dining room, she stopped and said with the same casualness. "Don't forget the lights when you're finished here. What's left of the liquor is over there beside the breadbox."

"I don't want anything more."

"No? Well, well. You *are* a changed man, aren't you?"

I made a slow and painful progress after her, conscientiously pushing switches—kitchen, pantry, dining room— as I went. I thought she'd gone straight upstairs, but when I reached the hall I found her standing at the bottom of the steps, waiting for me, her right hand on the newel post. During my search I'd put out, one by one, the lamps in the house, and she was in deep shadow. But I could see the white of her eyes in the light coming from the hanging lamp at the stair landing. "I want to make quite sure you understand me," she said. "I've had enough of every kind of lunacy"—her hand flew out in an inclusive gesture—"you're capable of."

I thought, of course, that we were back to Alma, but then, darker than the darkness around her, I saw the pedestal. It stood midway between Eleanor and the front door. In effect, it blocked her escape.

"But I——" I began protestingly. "If you mean . . ."

Her eyes flared, colder than any white fire of the hell she'd consigned me to. "I mean whatever you can think of."

I saw the immense thing stir, begin silently its slow, heavy turn. It aimed for her, not for me.

"Look out!" I said sharply.

"I shall. For myself, from now on. Only for myself. You can spare me your warnings. You need them more than I do." She started upstairs and then, after three or four steps, paused and leaned over the railing. "What made us think we could ever make a go of it?" she asked wonderingly. "Was it one of your delusions, dear, that slopped over on me?" The pedestal moved closer, but I felt sure she was safely beyond its reach. She leaned far out and ruffled my hair with her fingers. "Just think," she said crooningly. "From now on you can be as crazy as you like, and nobody will ever try to make you well again." She smiled and with her eyes half shut brought her right hand back to the railing and drew herself lightly upward. "Good night, love," she presently called down to me from the landing. "Good night."

I stood as she had left me for several minutes—or was it

only a second's fraction? Then, with my cripple's gait, I got myself round the newel post and lowered onto a step. I would sit my way up the flight.

I felt dizzy, and the darkness of the hall was particled with moving specks of light. I steadied my eyes and peered into that commotion. Surely the pedestal rose up a few feet before me? Surely I had watched it wheel toward my wife? Had she seen it, too? She must have, mustn't she? Wasn't that the particular "lunacy" she'd been referring to?—some notion I'd hauled it in here to document my fantasy. I tried to remember what she knew about the pedestal; how much, that is, I'd confided to her either intentionally or by unconscious allusion. But the effort took too much from me; and, besides, the illness I'd dreaded was hard at work in me. I could feel bitter waters on my gums; my tongue grew hard and swollen, a cruel reminder of the times it had pushed past Eleanor's lips and teeth and softened in her mouth. My stomach pressed against my belt with what had to be discharged, and in my throat the forerunner of that nasty mess stewed round, waiting for my will to falter. I lay back across the steps, closed my eyes, and kept perfectly still. Gradually, after minutes of plain physical hell, the bitter waters subsided, my stomach resumed its normal concavity, and I thought it safe to sit upright again. When I opened my eyes I discovered that I was in total darkness. Eleanor had shut out the landing light. I could not tell whether the pedestal was still before me or had gone back to its place. My knee hurt horribly—although, after this bout with internal disorder, such simple pain was almost comforting. But between that pain and the possibility that the sickness might return I had no desire to get up and hobble through night in search of . . .

Well, whatever it was: my enemy, my delusion, my terror, my death. Let it be my delusion, neatly settled now in the proper room of my brain until I called it out again.

I was shivering with cold and so, with a careful haste that regarded both stomach and knee, I began to haul myself upward. Since my eyes were useless, I closed them once more to prevent another bout of dizziness. I achieved the landing with a sense of relief more profound than I have felt in years, and I lay back briefly, breathing hard, clutching my shaking shoulders with my two warm hands. If I hadn't been so cold, I might have stayed there all night. If the damn' thing still stood down there in the hall, I was safe from it. It didn't know how to get up stairs. Was that, in fact, the reason it had moved tonight? With so many lights out, had it supposed we were in bed? Had it, that is, come out to practice? The comedy of the idea pricked my misery, my hopelessness, and I laughed through chattering teeth—perhaps aloud. I hauled myself upright and leaning heavily on the railing determined to get from here to bed as fast as possible. As I hung across the wood, face downward toward the blackness in the hall, I heard our door chimes jingle faintly, the way they do if someone walks heavily across the floor. When they died away my ears caught that familiar shuffle, that tiny scrape, the scratch of claws, the sigh, and finally that terrible, indescribable sound of something rising, swaying, revolving—of something formidably, unconquerably moving on.

# 18

I ROLLED sideways through morning sunlight to the edge of the bed and swung my legs out and downward. But as my feet touched the floor my lame knee sent its pain back through my thigh and I halted, was arrested, poised in an absurd posture on the side of the mattress. I turned gingerly onto my back and hoisted the sore leg, carefully, onto the sheet, and then closed my eyes, panting with the effort and the agony. It seemed scarcely a minute later that I heard footsteps in the hall. I'd pushed the sheet away, and now I grabbed it across me after a fashion—not soon enough, perhaps, for I heard Sarah say, "Oh! You're not up yet, Mr. Bayden. I was going to do the room."

"Later," I murmured, emulating a sleeper just aroused.

"Any time's fine," she assured me. "It's only I was here, was all."

"Thank you," I said. "I'll be out soon."

"Don't hurry." (Was she lingering?) "Some people!" she went on admiringly. "Talk about a soft life!"

"It's all that money, Sarah," I answered. "All that goddam money."

"That's as may be. Myself, I like to see a man taking his honest rest."

In desperation I said to her, "If you don't scram I'm going to get up and give you more honesty than you're ready for. I haven't got any pajamas on."

She giggled. "You think that's news? And tanned *all over!* I can't get Joe to even take his undershirt off outdoors." I heard the door creak slightly on its hinges, as if being drawn slowly shut. "Lucky we're all grownups here, isn't it?"

Finally, though I never heard the latch click, I felt sure she'd gone. With both hands supporting my knee, I got myself carefully out of bed and standing with the bedpost for support. The leg took weight better than I'd anticipated; I flexed it gently and after the initial fiery response the soreness almost seemed to diminish. An awkward choreography, involving bedpost, chair, chest, dressing table, brought me to the bathroom door. It was easy enough to get from there to the tub, and despite the fact that the day looked like being a scorcher I drew a hot bath and lay in it until sweat was streaming down my forehead and into my eyes. The knee responded well to heat and massage, and to a dose of strong linament that temporarily made a martyr of me all over again. My headache, ministered to with aspirin, retreated more slowly.

By the time I was dressed—in shorts and sandals—I was glistening with moisture as if I'd never toweled myself off. And I reeked like an old-fashioned cold. The day was not only hot but humid. Beyond the bedroom windows I could see the absolute stillness of the foliage in the woods down the slope. There wasn't even enough movement of air to bring into the house the almost overpowering sweetness of the pines which—like that of boxwood—is strongest on days like this one.

Downstairs was cooler; the sweat across my back began to evaporate. In the dining room I found my place had been set and I drank tepid apricot juice and ate cold cereal in warm cream. I yelled for Sarah and when she came in from somewhere across the hall asked her if she could make me toast and bacon. "I've bunged my knee," I said. "Otherwise, I wouldn't bother you. And Mrs. Bayden doesn't seem to be around."

"She got a taxi and went to town," said Sarah.

"Oh? Shopping? When was this?"

"A while back. An hour, maybe. Not long after I got here. I *guess* she was going to town. Shopping I don't know about. She looked pretty dressed-up for shopping."

My heart sank; I thought right away of a lawyer. But we don't deal with any of the local firms. And, anyway, whatever she proposed to do—if she proposed to do anything at all—surely she'd talk with me first.

Or would she? Do you discuss domestic adjustments or terminations with a hopeless mental case?

Though I was uneasy, I went on thinking that it was most unlikely she'd gone off to see a lawyer about a divorce or, even more drastically, upped and left me, carrying only —I could assume from Sarah's remarks—her purse. But where could she have gone, "pretty dressed-up"?

Sarah came back with the worst-looking bacon I've ever seen, and with toast that, very oddly, appeared to have been browned over a gas burner. There even seemed to be fork marks in it. These were accompanied, appropriately, by a stick of margarine with the foil carefully turned back at one end. I could scarcely believe that all of this glory had come out of our kitchen. Eleanor kept margarine for cooking, but there was almost a pound of butter in the keeper in the refrigerator door. As for the bacon, I'd bought the last lot myself, and hitherto it had not appeared at table looking gray, glistening, sluglike. More: the toaster had been working at least as recently as the previous morning.

"Thank you, Sarah," I said. "I know you've got plenty to do without bothering with this kind of thing."

"Oh, I love to cook."

I oleoed the toast, which was stiff and cold in my hand. The margarine rode across it in brave, unmelting ridges. Since, proud, solicitous, Sarah stood beside me, anxious to share my pleasure, I broke the slice into quarters and bit on one of them. After a time, a section yielded to my teeth and I worked away to get it down.

"I wonder if there's any coffee?" I said.

"I don't think so," Sarah replied.

I sipped water.

"I guess you heard," she went on.

"Heard?"

"They got a line on whoever it was killed the girl."

"What kind of line?"

"They don't say, naturally. But we're going to be surprised, they say."

"What 'they' this time?"

"Why, the people who say the other they have got a line on him."

"Since, as far as I can remember, I never laid eyes on the poor creature and never knew who her friends were, anybody they pick up will come as a surprise."

"Oh, but you understand what I mean."

"I guess I do. Somebody we've all heard of—somebody around here." She nodded. "I was told as much last night. We had a few people in——"

"I'll say you did!" She rattled with laughter.

I was slow. "That's right. You were here yesterday, too."

"Oh, that. Sure. But I meant you certainly *did* have a few people in!" The laughter came again. "And how!" She smiled broadly at me; we had, it seemed, a joke between us. I gave up the pretense of eating and apparently I looked my puzzlement, for she said, "You don't have to worry about its getting around. It's around already."

"It?"

"Naturally you don't want to say too much," she told me tolerantly. "But we all know she got it for good and all."

I began to have a horrible suspicion of what we were talking about. "And just how did it go around?" I asked.

She looked slightly abashed. "I don't know if it's all around *yet*," she said. "I heard it in the post office this morning. But they'll have it at Sparky and Ned's by noon."

The post office in Oldchurch—a large stone structure erected during the tenure of a United States senator whose hometown it shamelessly was—served as one of three local clearinghouses for late news. The other two were the grocery stores: Sparky's, which carried indifferently chosen but rather expensive wines, the only Dutch and Canadian beers for miles around, and a variety of unpleasing delicacies like chocolate-covered ants and deep-fat-fried grasshoppers, and Ned's, where villagers shopped for meat and vegetables. In any of these places one had only to stand and listen for ten or twenty minutes to gain a fresh sense of how marvelous is the imagination of the average no-nonsense adult. Rumor became indistinguishable from fact, libel from honest condemnation. It was nothing to find a woman at the far end of Ned's (picking up a package of what is now called "facial quality tissue") shouting across-store to a woman squeezing zucchini, "No, it was a bicycle chain. She took it off of one of the kids' bikes and went down to his place and started the minute he opened the door. He's going to lose the sight in one eye, they're afraid."

Into Sarah's happy, expectant silence I said, "You say she got it for good and all. Just how good, exactly?"

Sarah appeared puzzled and mildly impatient. "Well, how should I know *how* good? *You* know that! All I know is she's really had it as far as the town's concerned."

"I see. Even if the news isn't everywhere yet, it's reached quite a few people with remarkable speed."

"By eight-thirty a lot of folks have been in the post office at least once."

That, from all I'd heard, was true enough. Owl Hill was considerably beyond the corporation limits of the village, and we got our mail from the rural route carrier, but the post office and the grocery stores were subjects of hilarious gossip at all cocktail parties, and I was familiar with the extraordinary effectiveness of these media of communication. It would have taken the morning presence of only one of our last night's guests to start the news on its way.

"I think, Sarah," I said, "that this is one bit of gossip which ought to be played down. Mrs. Bayden would be distressed if she thought that a misunderstanding between friends had been magnified into a first-class row."

"Oh, no!" Sarah said cheerfully. "Right when she was going out, with the cab already waiting for her, she said to me, 'I really let her have it!'"

"Eleanor—Mrs. Bayden—said that?"

"Something *like* that. And her eyes sparkled. It does you a lot of good to get something off your chest—something you feel is really bad, especially, that you've been holding in on for personal reasons."

"I suppose it does. But . . . I hope you won't quote Mrs. Bayden among your friends?"

"No! Never! Oh, I'd never do that," said Sarah blithely. "If you'll excuse me now . . . I'm oiling that blamed big stick of wood of yours—every few days I pour it on, and every few days it's dry as a bone again. Those people didn't take care of it you bought it from."

"The pedestal?"

"Speaking of which," she said, "somebody's been pushing it back and forth. The floor's all scratched around it."

"The floor in the living room?"

My question was stupid, giveaway, but luckily she took it as an example of my wit and caroled her enjoyment. "Well . . . where *else?*" For a time the liveliness of our whole conversation kept her silent with laughter. "You mean it's been poking into other places?"

I smiled feebly. "That's no stranger than the idea that someone's pushing it around."

"I guess not. I'm only fooling, of course. The heels women have to wear now. My Lord, I've got scratch tracks on floors all over this house. Somebody'd been moving the thing around all night, if I started to blame it really. I thought you meant the joke everybody's passing around."

"Is there a joke about the pedestal?"

"*Is* there! And it's started up all the old talk about this place. Of course, folks have called this the haunted house since before ever I was born. Nobody takes it serious, exactly, but you'd be surprised the people you couldn't get to work here."

"Really?"

"My word on it. There's couples wouldn't even spoon in your drive—and that's going some in these parts, I don't have to tell you."

"Has the pedestal made things worse?"

"As for worse, who's to say?"

"I can't understand how stories got going in the first place."

"Everything gets talked about."

"Even the furniture in people's houses?"

"Everything. And that isn't exactly an ordinary piece of furniture. Though my guess is, it was Mrs. Bayden's finding you on the floor in front of it, knocked out cold, that stirred up interest."

"Is that how Mrs. Bayden found me?"

"Just what I said. I told everybody it wasn't one of my days. They couldn't prove it by me."

"Thanks for coming to our rescue."

The irony escaped her. "Loose talk does damage," she informed me. "You'll never hear me saying things I don't know for sure." With which piety she removed herself, permitting me to drag myself as quietly as possible to the lavatory off the kitchen, where I scraped my hideous breakfast into the toilet.

Afterward I put on a shirt and then got out the car and drove over to Oldchurch for cigarettes. It was almost noon by that time, and across the distances the landscape shimmered with heat. Midges wheeled skyward in ghostly chimneys. Our graveled drive sent up smoky plumes of dust as the car rolled over it. I turned out of the gates and followed the paved road down its long, crooked course into the valley—or "hollow," as it is commonly called. At the foot of our ridge the highway crosses Maryella's Run (a dry creekbed which, long ago, had briefly carried enough water for someone named Maryella to drown in), straightens out, and goes due east to the base of Oldchurch hill. Midway of that length is the new St. Peter's, on the north side of the road and set back from it perhaps three hundred feet. The former St. Peter's also stood on this site—during construction, we had held services in the basement of the Pythian Sisters' lodge in Oldchurch. What the Pythian Sisters made of the St. Peter's congregation was not more wonderful than what the congregation made of the ladies. We had parted at last with a kindly satisfaction on each side.

Ray and Alma lived in an oldish and pleasantly ugly house that was separated from the church by perhaps a half acre of lawn. It predated the period when the clergy began making it increasingly clear to congregations that the rectory-church complex was not, from the clerical point of view, a welcome one. A friend of mine in Cleveland insists that the minimum distance between church and priest's house should be fifteen miles, and he, in fact, lives about twenty away. Since, despite the urban sprawl, parishes retain something of their neighborhood character, he is spared the unexpected and undesired descent of parishioners with nothing better to do than make a call. ("They've always got some damn' problem," he says bitterly. "Usually it's what to do about the urine smell in the nursery, or how the goddam plants in the narthex are dying from lack of water. If we could stick the kids in the plants . . .")

Ray and Alma had complained often about the closeness

of the house to the church. St. Peter's was a tightfisted parish, however, as any association of moneyed people is likely to be, and until it got big enough so Ray could make a real case for getting an assistant I didn't see much chance of his unloading the old place on a flunky and settling somewhere farther away.

I braked the car slightly as I went past St. Peter's grounds. In good weather Ray's shabby old Volvo—which has a curious resemblance to a saleslady's black shoe—is never put away in the stables at the back, and its presence or absence in the oval before the house is almost an infallible sign of whether or not he's at home. On this morning it was gone, and I felt a strong desire to turn in and go to Alma. I had no idea what I could say, what there was to say, but I wanted very much, however I could, to protect her from the feeling of aloneness that I myself had. I imagined myself kissing her and handling her into quietness; I could feel my tongue gently moving on her salty eyelids and wetting and smudging the hair of her brows. I could even, in my sudden longing, feel the tiny, scattered lumps of whiteheads under the makeup on her face, those delicate hills that sometimes caught the lamplight or jumped out beneath the sun's hard look.

I braked; and then I drove on. If stories were already going around, my car outside the Gravatt house would do nothing to damp them down. No one could help Alma—so it seemed to me then. No man, at least, could help her without doing her further harm.

At the foot of Oldchurch hill the road turns suddenly to the south until it encounters the river (which, almost as suddenly, has turned north). Where they threaten to converge the road turns once again and begins to go upward.

Its course is leisurely and twisting, faithful perhaps to whatever wild-animal track was here to begin with. One mounts
through trees—the dying elms, the towering pin oaks, the
dogwoods that burn white in spring and fiercely red in
autumn. Some of the older people hereabouts still call the
dogwoods Jesus trees because of the legend that this
is the wood the Cross was made of. When autumn brings
out the bright red berries they say the Jesus tree is fresh
with blood before its dying—as, in spring, they say of the
white flowers that each shows the brown marks of Christ's
suffering for us all.

It is something of a shock to take the road's last rise and
curve and discover, at the summit, a village of clapboard and
white-painted brick. There is even, after a fashion, something like a New England green, on which the stores and
post office, the restaurant, and a few of the oldest houses
face. Some of the architecture is Greek Revival of an
economy order; some of it is chastened Victorian; there is
one exuberant example of Steamboat Gothic; and here and
there are traces of the Western Reserve. Oldchurch is far
from being the typical town to which farmers retire, but I
have never been able to learn what other motive might
have led to its establishment. For a time in the early part of
the nineteenth century it was, most improbably and auda-
ciously, the seat of Episcopal bishops; but the town was
here before the Church. And when the Church—that is to
say, the Church in its representative Presence—moved on,
the town continued modestly to flourish. The hotel where
people came for air had had its prosperity, but not enough,
one would have thought, to go all round. Even the name
for the place was a mystery. There was, to be sure, an old
church—a chapel, actually—just beyond the north edge of

the green, but it had been built in 1840-something, long after the erection of the original St. Peter's-in-the-Valley, and long after the naming of the town. The chapel was now abandoned, deconsecrated, its graveyard a place of tilted, eroded, unreadable, weed-shrouded stones. The origins of Oldchurch were similarly afflicted by time.

In the grocery store—Ned's, it was—I got a carton of cigarettes and then limped around picking up a few other small items. The voices of the village were all about me, and two in particular claimed my attention. From one I learned that "he"—the "he" could only be our murderer—was under twenty-four-hour watch. Who was watching him? her companion asked. Well, Albert Shardwell was helping out. (Albert Shardwell was an old drunk who'd once been mayor and now was on the grounds crew at the lodge. What kind of law officer would pick Albert to keep an eye on a suspected killer I couldn't imagine. But, then, Oldchurch was a looking-glass village, and often the reverse did happen here to what would happen any place else.) I knew no one in the store except Ned, who was cutting meat in the back, and the clerk, who was outside putting a box of groceries into the rumble seat of elderly Miss Wickers' vintage Pontiac. But I longed to ask exactly who it was Albert Shardwell was so keenly watching. As it happened, this penetrating question occurred to the second speaker, an ample woman with a flushed face who wore stretch jeans in pale pink and a blouse the color of curried chicken.

"What's he got to say?" she said. "Who is it?"

"Naturally," said her informant, "he don't tell everything he knows." She was a woman in build much like her companion; which is to say, like many of the local women

—like Sarah, in fact, to whom they were both probably related.

The stretch jeans vibrated, as if an irate stomach had popped them dangerously out. Their possessor said sharply, "Just like I thought. The only thing Albert Shardwell's watched in forty years is the level going down in a bottle."

"I'm just saying he *says* he is. He says it was an awful surprise to him."

I watched Miss Wickers offer her customary penny tip, totter aboard her Pontiac, and by an extraordinary series of dramatic gestures engage the engine's attention and spark it into life. She drove off the half-block to her house, her course obscured by exhaust smoke but clearly chronicled by ear-shattering explosions.

When I had withdrawn my attention from this ever-fascinating spectacle, I found that the two ladies had moved away toward the peat moss, lightbulb, and housewares section, where they were in murmuring conversation with several other customers. I saw a good deal of eyebrow tossing, some curious nose crinklings, and a few crosseyed squints, but I could make no sense of the random words that flew out as if expelled by the pressure of speculation. Then, as I was leaving, I felt in the curious way one does—along the neck and in the small of the back and down the thighs—that I myself had become an object of attention. I halted, scratched my head in pretended uncertainty, and turned toward housewares as if convinced I didn't have the frypan the little woman had especially asked for. Unfortunately, my knee gave a sharp twinge and my about-face may have looked like a lunge. The eyes of Albert Shardwell's historians were upon me, and they appeared startled, apprehensive. I could guess whose history they'd gone on to: *"that's* the one . . . wife really got her told . . . never try anything *else* around here. . . ." I halted with the weight on my good leg, peered into my bag, made noises of satisfaction, and started to leave again. The eyes had all dropped with the exception of stretch-jeans'. She, braver than her sisters, smiled sweetly at me and raised one hand in commiseration, congratulation, farewell.

# 19

THROUGH BRIGHT red leaves I saw them first, a man and a woman, seated together on a boulder halfway down the hillside. The rock maples bud and bloom this fresh-blood color, and then turn green as spring moves on. They are glory in the sunlight, but beneath an overcast they are the mind's affliction, a rage, a film across the eyes. On this blue day they were all gaiety and circus charm in the light breeze the afternoon had summoned. Around me in the woods were other flickers of red and blue, from cardinals and indigo buntings. Somewhere a thrush sang out and a crow made counterbass. Dead branches click-clacked faintly overhead, and the pine trees up the slope behind me made their hussing, burring song.

No, Sarah had said upon my return, Mrs. Bayden wasn't back and she hadn't called. No, nobody else'd called, either. If I didn't mind, she thought she'd leave a little early; there was an initiation at the lodge tonight, and everybody had to wear a formal. Hers needed pressing, among other things. Other things she had to do, that is. I told her to go along when she wanted to. My grasp of her problems gave me a small, secret amusement: I'd lived in the country long enough not only to share imaginatively in the complicated business of initiation but to know what a "formal" was. It was an elegance of either turquoise or pink taffeta, and it invariably cost $23.98.

As she was leaving the room, I thought of something I wanted to ask her. "By the way, Sarah. If they really think they're onto the man who murdered that hill girl, would they trust Albert Shardwell to keep an eye on him?"

"Albert Shardwell!" She hissed splendidly on his last name. "I could tell you things about Albert Shardwell you'd never believe."

"Yes, I would," I assured her.

"Worse than that, though. Those Shardwells are plain dirt. Anything anybody says they've heard him say about him is something he's made up. You mark my words."

Sarah's heavy reliance on pronouns and on the syntax of emotion no longer confused me. She meant that Albert Shardwell was a liar. He wasn't watching anybody—at least, he wasn't watching the murderer.

"I heard it in the grocery store," I explained. "In Ned's."

Sarah could not conceal her sophistication. "You can hear *any*thing in the grocery store!" she declared. She tittered. "Like Joe says, 'catch the fella bare-assed first.' "

She went away, borne off by laughter.

I no longer marveled, as I once had, at her fine inconsistency. I understood that the news one got at the grocery store or post office was valid only to the extent that one approved of its source. Perhaps those immense women with their springing flesh were not Sarah's kin, as

I'd suspected. Or, if kin, were not of the same social level. They, too, might be "dirt," to be crediting the likes of Albert Shardwell.

I made a late, scratchy lunch of cold meat and buttermilk biscuits from last night's dinner. Regularly—and, as a rule, just as I was swallowing—a panic caught my stomach: where *was* Eleanor? Three hours, four hours, almost five by now. I gave up midway of the second biscuit and fired what was left of it out the kitchen door for the birds to finish. Then I drank a glass of ice water and went slowly, with the limp I seemed by now to have had all my life, toward the living room. Sooner or later I had to look at the pedestal. I had to see it back in its place—that blamed big stick, as Sarah called it, which would glisten in the sun with the coat of oil it had got today. With the knowledge of its power I'd acquired so recently, I wanted to confront it in daylight. I wanted to see what it could contrive to do in an ordinary hour.

Sarah was on her knees before one of the living-room sofas, a pail of sudsy water beside her. She was scrubbing away at the fabric of a seat cushion. "Somebody sure spilled *some*thing here last night," she said, panting. "I hate to think what."

"Gin, rye, bourbon, or Scotch," I answered absently.

"*Blood*'s what I'd of guessed," she said, and tittered again.

I hobbled past her—profoundly grateful for her presence—but I couldn't bring myself to go the full length of the room, to confront the pedestal directly. I halted at last beside an overstuffed chair, and after a moment of indecision—what, exactly, should I do next?—lowered myself to its arm. The pedestal showed its slick still; I thought it looked less in need of oiling than a brutal washing in hot, soapy water. Suppose we were to send it out to be refinished like any other scratched and dented piece. Suppose I hauled it down to my workshop and, after sealing its stain with aluminum paint, coated it with bright pink enamel. Suppose we sawed off its lower third, made that the support for a lamp table, and junked the rest of it. In short, what could indignity accomplish?

But my imaginings lost heart before its utter quiescence. It was no more inimical than the sofa Sarah was scrubbing, or any other piece of furniture in the room. It was, in fact, just that: a piece of furniture. In that moment I simply could not believe that it moved through my nighttime house. I marveled at the composure Ray had shown when I brought out my fantastic story.

In short, confronted by the pedestal—I who had come to confront—I became deeply uncertain of what I had seen. Surely I hadn't moved it into the hall, in the dark of the present day, as a strike at Eleanor. Had I? Even if I had, with my bad knee I hadn't got up before dawn and moved it back. For my knee was certainly injured; the pain would have waked me. Wouldn't it? Had I not fallen quite by accident, and hurt myself considerably?

Is it the same for everyone—the horror of a secret life? The vivid dreams one has, detailed, chronological, with no ellipses . . . Does everyone wonder whether these are promptings of a secret life, things that pass as dreams until the final, dreadful waking? For my generation, there is that story of the French detective who set out to find a murderer and discovered himself. I have felt myself he a thousand times, but do I really take his terrible course?

*Every kind of lunacy you're capable of,* Eleanor's voice

said in my brain. *I've had enough. I've had enough. . . .*

"You folks ever going to decorate that thing?" Sarah asked from behind me.

Blessed woman! She broke the spell. I got myself upright and turned round toward where she still knelt beside the sofa—the job evidently done, however, for she was blotting the fabric with a towel.

"Someday," I said to her. "Any ideas?"

"Ideas mean more work," she answered, "and I can't take heights. How about one of them clocks in glass cases?"

"Why not?" I laughed like anyone newly freed of anxiety. "Talk it over with Mrs. Bayden." I limped past her toward the hallway door.

"You ought to see a doctor," she said.

"I'll be all right. I've seen enough doctors for a while."

"Well, I knew a man had a hoe handle fly up and hit him, and you know what?"

"He hit it back?"

"Laugh as long as you can. He died of a cancer it give him."

"I could stand to die from cancer. It would almost be a relief."

"Just don't say you wasn't warned. I have to go soon, like I told you."

"I remember. Have a good time at your initiation."

"I'll likely hear who it is."

"Who what is?"

"You know. The fella killed that girl. It'll be all around, if it's already got to Albert Shardwell."

"Oh," I said. "Yes, I suppose it will. If Albert Shardwell's watching him, even . . ."

[ 96 ]

"Ex*actly*," said Sarah, mopping vigorously. "And just like I said, isn't it?"

"I don't know. Is it?"

"I mean, somebody we all know. Prominent. *That's* the only kind they wouldn't put in jail first and ask questions afterwards."

"I suppose you're right."

"I *know* I am. All them fancy airs . . ."

"Is he fancy?"

Sarah tossed her head. "Is he ever! And that mealy-mouthed way he has."

I said on an impulse, "I dare you to speak his name straight out."

"Ah! That there's slander. Thank you very much."

"You don't know, you mean."

"I got my suspicions. Oh, yes! I could name one or two and be pretty close. You give me a call late tonight."

"And what if I really do?"

"Well!" She bridled and flushed pink. "I guess I'll have a thing or two to tell you."

That's when I went outdoors and walked slowly toward the pine grove. Every step was painful, yet I couldn't have borne to sit in the house. Later, I thought, I'd go swimming; that would be excellent therapy for my knee. But at this hour the pool still caught the sun's full light, and the day was so miserably hot and airless that only some place shady would be endurable. Beneath the pines the temperature was perceptibly lower and I stretched out on my back and closed my eyes and tried for a time to forget about last night, to forget Eleanor's mysterious absence—even to forget this man, this killer, whose identity seemed so close to being known. Why the nearness of this revelation should fill me with something very like panic I couldn't have said. I was, perhaps, the more frightened because there seemed no reason to suppose that he would be more than a name to me, if he managed even to be that. I didn't really believe that Bob Fruig or someone equally familiar had been the girl's lover. There was, to begin with, the problem of proximity; rather, of lack of proximity. These hill people are not easily met. It would be a most unusual set of circumstances that would make possible a sustained relationship with one of them—and I didn't think that the girl's job at the restaurant in Oldchurch could have provided those circumstances. That is a place one goes to with reservations, wife, friends—and dressed up and fully and pleasantly in the public eye. There are plenty of bars in the town west of us where associations can be formed, but the hill people appear in these places, I suspect, as seldom as our friends do. Both of us, in our different ways, would be conspicuous and uncomfortable. And, inevitably, there would be talk. Plainly, of that sort of talk there was none; we should have got our full of it last night, if there were, or for days past from Sarah.

Nor was my deep unease the result of a suspicion that, like the French detective, it was really myself who sheltered at the heart of the mystery. Eleanor kept—had kept—close watch on me. There was no slightest chance of the kind of liaison that, surely, must require large parts of afternoons or evenings, or even hours into the night; that, more, must rely on a plausible schedule of deception. Lacking any schedule at all, I was seldom gone from the house for long, except when Eleanor was with me. Any considerable absence would have had to be explained (it was not so much infidelity that she feared as the possibility of my having a fit and making a scene somewhere).

The girl's death had troubled me since we first got news of it: as evidence of violence unleashed, bearing down on all of us. Now she herself was forgotten, a woman nobody had known (when had her funeral been? where was she buried? who were her mourners and what had become of the children?). The excitement continued to mount, but it had redirected itself toward her murderer—who just might, with luck, turn out to be somebody's dearest friend, some place's leading citizen. The situation had the homely reality of a certain kind of nightmare, in which the comfortably familiar becomes the chuckling evil, and the brain fights the madness attendant on incredulity, on trust betrayed.

So I lay on my back, in murmuring, scented coolness, and fought my panic, my sense of something awful soon to be known, soon to infect us with a dreadful passion, a fatal sickness. And then at last, defeated, I got up. I stumbled down the slope, past the final row of pines, and into the hardwoods. There was no sense to my direction; I went on wounded leg as gravity indicated, and without a thought for the hard climb up again. Where a windfall blocked my path I halted: it was an oak whose great hollow base I and my sister and cousins had played in as children; a tree so delightful that had I had child of my own I would have called in surgeons to save it for whatever imaginings my son might possess. I hauled myself onto it, and looked farther down the slope through the bright red tender leaves of maples, and saw the lovers seated close together.

They were beautiful in the light that filled their clearing, the woman all gold and gleam beneath the sun, the man a substantial semidark beside her. They did not touch, but in their bodies' lean I thought I saw that comfortable assent that comes after fierce embraces. I loved them for what seemed to be their love, and for the splendor they gave this ominous day. From my lonely eminence I sent them benediction. Our woods—and hence our lives—were good for something, if they brought a man and woman close together. I thought of the people who perpetually dance in sunlight in the permanent gardens of Arcadia. It was that mythic quality that I attributed to the hillside below me. All loveliness and holiness; grace abounding. I could return to this place tomorrow and find them still engaged in their timeless drama: two lovers in a pastoral, utterly touching, utterly unrelated to the hard life of the higher slopes. They were consolation and rest; they were even hope.

I did not, you see, care who they were or where they came from or whether this woman could honestly claim this man. I did not think to question whether their meeting was clandestine, merely discreet, or tragically ill-advised. I was content to share their enchantment. I am a naïf—the doctors say it is part of my illness—and the joy I think I see calls out a similar joy; I cannot be critical of happiness. I never think to be suspicious of love, or even of the gestures of friendship. And so, it seems, from too much faith I wound, and in my own turn am wounded worse.

With what was surely unnecessary caution, since my approach hadn't been heard, I slid off the trunk and prepared to retreat up through the pines and onto the lawn. Then it struck me, belatedly, that this was rather a cool pair. True, the gate in the wall along the river road is never bolted when any of the family is in residence, and the upper gates, which lock electrically, are not closed until night—and, at that, only when we remember to push the master switch in the closet under the back stairs. Through one or the other of these entrances anyone can come onto Owl Hill at any time he chooses. For that matter, even when the main entrances are shut an agile man or woman can vault the utilitarian chainlink fencing that runs down either side of the property, connecting the more stately barriers along each frontage. But why would anyone risk the possible embarrassment of being caught trespassing merely to sit in our woods? The trees go on to the west of us, and, since our nearest neighbors on both roads are almost a mile away, the area is virtually unpatrolled. We have occasional visitors who want to know what it "really looks like" behind these walls and gates and woods and masking pines, but most of them are quite polite and motor at a funeral pace to our front door, where they descend and ring the bell.

I had already turned away and taken a couple of steps up the hill when simple curiosity got the better of me. Who *were* these radiant people who used our land as theirs, and with such assurance that I was perfectly routed? I crept slowly back, feeling indecent, like a voyeur, and leaned across the fallen tree and peered down, squinting hard as shortsighted people always do for maximum focus. Through the red blur of leaves I made them out, but still not plainly. Though his hand was on her golden shoulder, I couldn't decide whether he was amorous or consolatory. At any rate, she didn't respond. She drooped away from him and seemed to lower her face onto her drawn-up knees. The sunlight glinted on her brilliant hair, her fragile nape. And he, as if in irritation, stood up abruptly, jumped off the boulder, and swung round to confront her.

Ray.

And the woman who lifted her head then was, as I think

I had known but refused to believe for some seconds, my wife. Or had I really guessed this when I first saw them together? Was my "curiosity" an improvisation of the unconscious mind? At any rate, the use of our woods was now explained.

Had they met here other times? Was the arrangement suspect merely because it was unusual? Ray had told me he was Eleanor's confidant, and pointed out that he was the proper person for her to go to. And possibly her feeling about Alma—which last night must have reached a culmination, not a sudden, illogical turning—had made it difficult for her to go to the church. To go to the church was to go to the rectory; it appeared there was something to be said for the separation of the two on the parishioner's side, as well.

All this I tried to think. I tried to be fair. But I was sick with jealousy, sick with hurt. I yearned above them—I would have taken gratefully any slightest favor either sent me. I felt betrayed and betrayed—by my brain and body's love, by my spirit's longing for gentleness and compassion and understanding. My wife and my priest. My harsh-tongued, intolerant wife who was the beautiful companion of my flesh; my stupid priest who was the one God's living presence in my life.

He still stood—furious, it seemed—before her, hands on his fleshing hips. And she, with the quick grace I knew so well, jumped up and off the rock, gestured in the general direction of the house, and vigorously shook her head. So they stood for moments that passed for me like minutes, and which were terrible because I wondered how they would conclude.

In effect, they did not conclude. Eleanor turned away

abruptly and started downhill, and after a moment Ray followed her. I watched them descend single file beyond my sight. They were gone into the blur of red, the bloody maples, the blood of their slaying. For rage succeeded gentler feelings, and I dreamed of violent death for both of them.

# 20

SARAH'S BRIGHT red Sunbeam—which she closes herself into through a combination of dexterity and magic—was gone when I re-emerged on the lawn. My knee was throbbing badly and it was a difficult business getting back to the house. But in a happier, more reformatory time we'd cleared out the bar in the pool house, in order to discourage me from tippling in midmorning or early afternoon, and I needed a drink at least as much as I needed to exercise my leg in water. I made it finally and ascended that same interminable flight of steps on which I'd fallen about twelve hours earlier. In the kitchen I assembled glass, ice cubes, and a half-empty bottle of bourbon from the collection that still stood beside the breadbox. I pitched all of them together into our fifty-four-cent Styrofoam cooler, which is so incredibly much more efficient than those we have in silver and brass, or our insulated picnic buckets covered with leather, and went out and down again.

The sun still fell across a part of the pool, but the deeper end lay in shade. I poured a long drink and then sat down and began slowly to take my clothes off. I was so tired my hands shook, and I wished I'd put on a pullover shirt rather than one that had to be laboriously unbuttoned. I didn't have a jock on, and the zipper on my shorts caught in the hair of my belly and the pain sent a fire through my loins. When I stood up, naked, I was almost erect, and the water in the shaded part of the pool made me hard as murder. I scarcely noticed how the pain in my leg was diminishing. Or perhaps I did in an obverse way, by my awareness of returning vigor. I could have rutted anything. I understood the deep necessity of rape, and for that time it seemed to me better that a woman should be roughly violated than that a man should endure the kind of mental as well as physical hell that blinds him to every other matter of his own or the public life. Since the short business of propagation is all that is required of men, why should they not be the difficultly roused, and women the ardent seducers? Instead, each man lives in an agony of fuck. Every day issues its imperatives, and he is helpless to ignore them.

In that time of terrible sexual pain, of deep human need, I surfaced and saw kneeling on the tiled lip of the pool the woman I held most beautiful, most lovable, most splendid and fine. I swam quickly over to her, to hide myself against the tiles, feeling suddenly as embarrassed as a teen-ager with one of those involuntary erections that make shy boys go on sitting after the class bell sounds.

"Turn your back," I said, "and I'll go in the pool house and put a pair of trunks on. I wasn't expecting anybody."

"No. I won't stay. I tried the house. I thought both of you might be down here. I wanted to talk to Eleanor." I almost said, Eleanor's in the woods with your husband. "I suppose you know what happened?"

I wiped my eyes with my fingers and pushed the hair

back from my face. "I know you had a row with her—but I did, too, and in the commotion I didn't get many details."

"I wouldn't have come today—or ever again," she went on. "But for Ray's sake we've got to put a face on it. Things are bad enough. That girl . . ."

"Alma." With the hand that didn't support me at the edge of the pool I touched her knee. "It needn't be a 'face.' It shouldn't be, among the four of us. Eleanor's——"

"Upset." She smiled wryly, showing a tooth daubed red from a too hasty application of lipstick. "I know. You told me last night. But you rather skimped on the reasons for Eleanor's distress." She looked so haggard and hopeless and brave that my hand tightened on her knee in a spasm of love and affection. If I had been a bolder man with two sound legs I would have swung myself out of the water and taken her in my arms.

Instead, like the fool I was, believing that something remained to be saved, I said, "I'd better get dressed."

She gently removed my hand, stood up, and shook her head. "I must go. It would be worse . . . Will you ask her?"

"I'll damn' well tell her."

Alma managed a faint laugh. "That might have helped the two of you a few years ago. It won't help any of us now. No. You've got to persuade her that what she does to me she does to Ray. You must put it on a practical basis. That's all she'll understand. And thank you, Johnny. I didn't want . . . It's wrong to drag you into this. It's really something for the three of us to settle."

She walked quickly away, climbed the broad, shallow steps to the lawn, and disappeared beyond the tall hedge of boxwood that rims the pool's upper side.

*The three of us.* They had shut me out—not just now but at some earlier time. They had closed upon one another in a ferocious contest for which I was ineligible. Because I was too sick? The reason didn't matter any longer—to me any more than to them. I was now the involved outsider, set free by their will to evolve my own rules, to settle the game after my choice with no consideration of theirs. And by Christ that's what I'd do.

So, in less than an hour, I'd gone from murderous rage to sexual frenzy to rage again. The emotions succeed each other easily, of course, and in my case were inflamed by my sense of betrayal. More, I was humiliated: to lose what one has loved is terrible enough; to lose what one has looked down on and patronized is to have the guts themselves snatched out.

I got very drunk and then, in the dying light, I walked slowly back to the house and climbed the long flight to the kitchen. From there I paced the whole ground floor and listened at the front staircase. If Eleanor had come in, she was either up there asleep or moving around with caution. Finally, I went to the living room and lay on a sofa near my old enemy, my friend, my strangely ambulatory possession. The pedestal. For a while I slept.

# 21

My GRANDFATHER'S library is a big room at the front of the house on the ground floor. As every proper library ought to be, it is shelved on all four walls, except for space left for doorway, chimney, and two windows, one looking onto the porch, the other westward toward the pine grove. Some of my happy memories are connected with the walnut and brass ladder that runs round the room on wheels, attached at its top to a metal pipe track that stands out about a foot from the cases and some three feet below the ceiling. My sister and I and our cousins used to perch on the top rung—whichever among us had got there first, that is—through the hot, boring, blissful summer afternoons of childhood, playing a form of king on the mountain while the others jiggled the ladder ferociously on its rubber wheels or pushed it along its track at a dizzying speed. This game being notorious, it seldom lasted more than five minutes before an adult came in to scold us and send us outdoors. Other times, particularly when my parents and my sister and I were the only guests at Owl Hill, I used to retreat to the ladder's top to do my dreaming: that I was one of the Hardy Boys, and on the verge of discovering an important clue, or that I was Poppy Ott, about to produce another invention (his pedigreed pickles so moved me that for a month or more I planned to give my whole life to the cucumber). The ladder was no prop to a rich man's ego, nor was it a decorator's idea of proper library furniture. Though my grandfather spent most of his time in his Edgewater Drive house, Owl Hill was where he proposed to retire, and he always came here with a load of books in the trunk on the luggage carrier or in a box on the back seat. Gradually, shelves filled up—from those impossible ones that run round just above the floor, and are always blocked with furniture, to the highest which only the ladder makes practicable. During the last years of his life my grandfather was perpetually engaged in "weeding," and, since sentiment so often overrode sense, we have almost as many shelves in the upstairs study, where more of the weeded went than ever landed in the furnace or garbage pit. (I am talking in the main of a time before one automatically sent discarded books to parish rummage sales, nursery school bazaars, hospitals, and the more literary prisons.)

That study is just above the library, and has the same dimensions and the same high ceiling. The only real difference, aside from the quality of literature on display, is in the bookcases, which are less than eight feet high. Above, the walls are decorated with huge sepia engravings—all, as nearly as I can make out, perpetrated by somebody named Axel Haig in the year 1908. I keep wishing for a few hand-tinted photographs by Wallace Nutting, but I suppose he is too "late." Axel Haig was very strong on massive, ornamented cathedral fronts, and soaring ecclesiastical interiors with unlikely reredos or roodscreens. A chill wind whips across all of his representations. To look up when entering the study is to suffer acute, instant clerical frostbite. Happily, to look down is to encounter the endearing fictional simplicity of the first forty years of this century. Here, as if borne from the library to the study by their own light weight, are some of the popular books of that time: *The Tin Soldier* and *The Blue Window* by Temple Bailey; *Spring Came On Forever* by Bess Streeter Aldrich; *The Turmoil* by Booth Tarkington; *Lovey Mary, Young Felix, The Awakening of Helena Ritchie,* and *Poor Dear Margaret Kirby; Summer Bachelors* by Warner Fabian and *Whither* by Dawn Powell; *Anne of Avonlea; The Enchanted April* and *The Adventures of Elizabeth in Rügen;* Howells' *Vacation of the Kelwyns; Janet March, The Red Lamp, The Duchess of Wrexe, The Young and Secret.* . . . I did so beautifully in my bedtime games—all the titles you can think of that use "blue," fifty novels by Patricia Wentworth—because I'd read almost everything in this room and, from either enthusiasm or morose curiosity, other works by the same authors.

I go over these books with something of the devotion of a man telling his beads. It is an act of celebration and an act of grief: I celebrate the delightful life they seemed to promise me, and I mourn my failure to achieve it—the failure of all of us, perhaps, to inhabit a golden world of laughter and tenderness and love. These books once gave me my best happiness; sometimes I think they have given me my only enduring happiness.

I had waked from my nap feeling drugged, stupid, tired out from rest I didn't really need. My watch was down at the pool, forgotten when I'd put my clothes back on, but the erratic Regency tall-case clock in the hall held its elegant hands at six-fifteen—which meant that the hour was somewhere between half-past five and seven. I yelled up the stairs to Eleanor and then hobbled back toward the kitchen, calling her. The clock on our electric stove—the only accurate timepiece in the house—said it was six-forty-five. I felt the panic again: she'd been gone almost nine hours. *Had* she left me? (But does a woman who has deserted her husband make an appointment the same day to meet another man on her husband's grounds? —Doesn't she, rather, get as far away as possible, or at least get to where she's going, and from there begin to call round her her friends and counselors? I couldn't be sure; Eleanor first, and then the doctors, had told me that my notions of common sense were part of my illness. That is, my sense was no one else's.)

If I'd been absolutely sure she was gone, I'd have felt something very close to relief. Not that I didn't then think that I still loved her and wanted her to go on being my wife. But we had come to a point where talking was very difficult, where lovemaking was impossible, and the memory of it so beautiful and beautifully free of complications that it made the present situation unbearable. I marveled that I could have handled her so boldly, this stranger that she was now. One summer day, soon after our engagement, we'd come down to Owl Hill for the afternoon and walked in rain, naked under our raincoats, and with a hand in each other's pocket—the kind of pocket that opens on the inside. My seeking hand had found her body as hers found mine, and blissfully, awkwardly we'd bumped along to the pine woods where I stripped her bare and lay on her wet, shivering body and took her fast. And then I held until she came too, and after that I was still hard, wild with excitement, and gently, sweetly she put her mouth to me. I loved her with all my heart; I thought we would be happy forever. I believed that nothing could ever seriously affect the relationship of two people who gave each other such delirious joy, who could be utterly wanton because they were utterly committed. She let me go and passionately I licked the fragile length of her; I worshiped the budding bristles on her legs, the cheese of dirt between her darling toes. She was all over pine needles and pitch, dirt and sex: my adorable, smudgy-nosed, sticky-cunted girl.

And now, in a way I didn't understand, for a reason that belonged rather to the beginning or midpoint of my illness than to its termination, she had become my enemy. I was aware of a rising fear of her, of what she might do to me. What had she said to Ray? What was she telling other people? Our bodies' joy had no immortality. We were free to rise, brush ourselves off, and commit a harsh treason. Did she wish me back in that immaculate sanitarium?

I'd had nothing to eat since my meager, pickup lunch, and my head was aching again either from liquor or from the lack of sufficient food. I boiled water for coffee and made toast which I ate standing at the sink. So far did habit still persist that I told myself I didn't want to spoil my dinner—that dinner which of course my wife would get me.

It was now just past seven, and outdoors the light held steady. I considered calling some of our friends, to ask whether Eleanor had stopped round by one of them for a drink. But if she hadn't . . . There was talk enough going on; I didn't want to add to it unnecessarily. Ray? She might have told Ray where she was going when they parted. And surely, by this time, they *had* parted? No, I couldn't bring myself to speak to him. Though Eleanor found it possible to meet him face to face within hours of having denounced his wife, this smaller act of telephoning him was more than I could manage. Perhaps because, it seemed to me then, I bore her shame as well as my own. She could hardly understand the wound it is to have the wife of your heart and body so cruelly treated. Once, not long before my worst collapse, my sister, who has never liked Eleanor, turned on her with a similar shrill fury, blaming her for my illness, for our lack of children, for the joyless frenzy of so much of our life. I was stricken; I could not bear to hear my love so harshly attacked. It was worse because it came from someone whom I also loved—and Ray was not without feeling where we were concerned. As our priest, surely he at least cherished Christ's love for us. I grieved for him, for Alma, for my wife who did not know what she had done.

The coffee and toast made me hungrier, but I rinsed out my cup and held the butter knife under the hot water, and then I went back to the front of the house. I stood on the porch for perhaps ten minutes, listening anxiously for the sound of a car slowing down in the road, turning into the drive. No false hopes were raised, for no traffic went by at all. The evening was breathlessly hot and perfectly still: the daybirds had settled, the owls had not yet risen.

I went indoors and upstairs to the study—the room, as I've indicated, of my comfort and distraction. But I could settle to none of my old friends. Their jackets, I saw, were faded; their authors were almost all dead; their paper was growing brittle, some of it was yellowing, and here and there a binding had succumbed to mildew. And the texts performed no magic for me: the scattered sentences I read revealed instead the sad grasp of grammar and punctuation, the prompt resort to cliché, that I could usually ignore.

*Why have you fled from me, Alice Grant Rosman? . . .*

I sat down at the desk I had had moved in here when we came back to stay—the library, for the life of his house, will be my grandfather's—and it was then that I began this narrative. I used the elderly standard typewriter we'd found in the basement and had reconditioned, and I wrote on sheets cut from a stained roll of shelving paper that had spent a good many years under the sink: like all rich people, we practice pointless, laborious thrifts. It had taken me almost the whole of an afternoon to reduce the roll to a ream of paper approximately nine by twelve. On the other hand, I had nothing else to do; and perhaps this was the equivalent of my grandfather's custom of walking from Cleveland's Public Square up nine blocks of Euclid Avenue to his office in order to save the two-cent streetcar fare. Don't buy what you already have, and never pay for what you can do yourself. The economies are bred in the bone.

I began my narrative at random—with the purchase of the pedestal (but was that, really, the random beginning it seemed to me at the time?). Then I jumped to Sarah, and from Sarah to Owl Hill and the life of this township and county. Since then I've added, patched, and shuffled pages, trying for some coherent progression. But on that first evening I had no intention of telling the tale of Eleanor and me, Ray and Alma, and a girl shot dead back in the hills. The engrossment hadn't yet come upon me; I was, just then, writing to fill up time, and with the vague idea that a thing committed to the page—even the typewritten page—loses some of its personal horror. Psychodrama on paper, you know. The loonies who attend us have a great idea there. Or did a patient suggest it first?

There's only one trouble: to what extent does the drama

take on a life, a course, of its own? Does it simply mirror with, perhaps, an exaggerated brilliance, as a luster in fire-light is more fire than fire itself? Does it run parallel, not quite the same as the original because it is either shallower or deeper, but always going the same route, ending the same way? Or does it, at some point, radically diverge?—so that we have finally to say of it: This is an event in itself; what really happened may have been less, may have been more, but certainly was different. The question, of course, is one that whoever reads this must settle for himself.

I had been working for almost an hour when I heard the tap of heels along the hall, the sound of the door just opposite being opened and a light switched on. The room was my grandmother's, where Ray and I had talked early this morning. I pushed back my chair and got quickly to my feet, despite the protest of my game knee, and then, very quietly, almost stealthily, I sat down again. I knew quite well that Eleanor was out there: every woman's walk is different. And I knew, as surely as if my desk were in line with the door and I could see what was happening, that she was moving out on me. The footsteps sounded again in the hall, went along to our bedroom. I heard drawers being pulled out, pushed shut. Presently, the steps returned: I could see her perfectly in my imagination, arms filled with panties and bras, stockings and nightgowns. All the things I had so lovingly given her, so joyously taken off her.

In my grandmother's room a reluctant drawer came open with the thin crack of distant gunshot. And through a window I heard, deep in the woods below me, the first excited barking of the owls.

# 22

SHE WAS stuffing clothes away without any sense; her face was pink and a line of sweat showed across her forehead. There was a scratch on her right leg, and both shoes were pale with dust.

She said, "All right. You can see, can't you?"

"I've waited dinner for you."

"Too bad. I've had mine."

"You might have phoned."

"I might."

"You might also have let me know you were going off for the day."

She straightened herself, drew the back of a hand across her forehead, and laughed. "You forget. I'm finished with you. I don't owe you anything—not a note, not a phone call."

"Then why not move all the way out?"

"At present, I have my reasons."

"All right. I'll accept that, because I've mine for overlooking your behavior."

She looked at me with a surprise that was succeeded by anger. "Behavior! *You* are lecturing *me* about *behavior?*"

"As long as you live in my house you'll conduct yourself in a way that causes neither of us embarrassment."

"Don't worry yourself. I'm leaving enough stuff behind, including the things on my dressing table, so Sarah will never know I'm not sleeping there. And I'm keeping the door of this room locked—not just against Sarah, however."

My concern hadn't, of course, been Sarah, or the tales she'd spread if she got wind of our separation—though I was relieved to learn that I had one less problem to cope with. I was trying to lead round to the subject of the quarrel with Alma and the necessity of the four of us putting up a convincing appearance of friendship.

"Do you plan to stay long?"

She picked up a couple of dresses that lay across the mattress and carried them over to the closet. "I don't know, I can't tell." She went quickly back to my grandmother's dressing table and began rearranging the contents of a drawer.

I don't believe in the kind of pride that is merely the exalted sense of self, the self that never lowers or bends, that stores up injustices, omissions, and calculated malices until these become its sour essence. I felt, abruptly, overwhelmed by the extent of our estrangement. If I could bring her back to me, I was more than willing to humble myself.

So: "I love you," I said. I stood, as I had since the beginning of our interview, just within the door, and I made no move toward her. "However I've behaved, whatever I've done to make you unhappy, I've never lived a minute of any day without the sense of you. You have a house in the middle of my forehead. Do you believe me?"

"I think I do."

"Today. Sure I was sore not to know where you were, but more, much more than that, I was worried. I can't stand thinking something might happen to you. Do you believe that, too?"

She was bent above the drawer. "I was all over," she mumbled tonelessly. "I got my hair done—can't you tell? And then . . . ." She shut the drawer hard, went over and propped herself, back toward me, against the wardrobe in the corner. "I had lunch. Early. To give me time to walk back out here along the river road to meet Ray." She swung round, with that declaration, and I did my best to emulate surprise. "I called him this morning and asked him to meet me in the woods. There were . . ." She shrugged. "Things," she said. "Afterward I came back to the house and called a taxi and went into town again. You were out somewhere. I saw the last part of a movie. Then I had dinner. I walked over to the library and picked out some books to bring back and suddenly I didn't want any of them. Philena Thorne"—one of the two reference librarians—"called a cab for me."

"All this . . . just to keep out of my way, keep me out of your sight?"

"All right, since you insist on asking: to keep you out of my sight, yes. Except the Ray part."

"And what about him?"

Her eyes dropped. "Nothing."

"You walked nearly four miles out from town just for nothing?"

"I had to see him."

I went over to the mattress where I'd sat hours before and resumed my former position, and once again I felt myself slipping into the role of suppliant. "You've done a bad thing by him," I began. "You may have ruined him here. Did he tell you any of this?"

She'd gone quite pale. "You're wrong. I haven't—— You're crazy. He'd have said something. *How* am I supposed to have ruined him?"

"By talking too much. You've said some vicious things to Alma, and anything you say against her is a knock against Ray. The story about last night is all over Oldchurch. And before Sarah's finished with it it'll be over the whole county."

I'd expected more temper in response to this, or at the least an angry justification, but she looked merely thoughtful. She walked across to a window at the front of the room and opened it. A small breeze lifted her hair and shook it gently. "You're right, of course," she said.

"And you know, I suppose, that he's in something of a spot over the murder of that hill girl."

"Is he?" Her voice was dead level, but strangely she'd gone tense all over. I was reminded of Alma's conduct at the party, the abrupt way she left Sybil Fruig and me when we began talking about the killing. It's impossible to guess what kind of event will deeply disturb a woman and what kind she will be indifferent to, and the problem isn't a simple one of categories: murder yes, robbery no. I wondered whether there was something about the dead girl that each responded to, made an identification with. And that the girl had had children, and they themselves had none . . . Might this also come into it? I didn't know; I could only be sure that, for whatever reasons, this remote murder was not done with where we were concerned.

I said, "I'm merely making the point that he's got enough on his hands already, without having to cope with a feud."

"Yes." She swung one leg up on the windowsill and hunched down on it listlessly, her face still half-turned away from me. "I suppose you think I ought to go see her."

"No. That is . . . I don't really know. I haven't thought that far. Didn't Ray have any . . . suggestions?"

A smile curled the corners of her mouth. "Oh, yes."

"Well?"

"You'd have approved their air of propriety. But they won't help out where Alma's concerned."

I knew, even then, that the conversation had gone astray; women are always charmed to lead you gently off the track, especially if they believe that you're innocent of the new direction. But I was still far too unsuspecting to guess what a wilderness she'd drawn me into. And because the trick is both irritating and offensive, I determined to ignore it.

"Then we'll have to work this out on our own hook," I told her. "Nothing too obvious, of course."

"Of course."

"We'll think of something."

"You will, I'm sure. You're wonderfully inventive where Alma's concerned."

"*You* are, you mean," I answered, and I felt such a surge of anger that I could have struck her. It seemed as if we were trapped again in the same pointless debate—and I was so weary of it that I had nothing except violence to bring out as my rebuttal.

For a moment, in the way she turned her face toward me, in the rigid stalk of her neck, I thought she meant to flare back. But she said, quite mildly, "I think we've talked as much as we can, for now."

That was eminently reasonable, and I accepted it. "All right," I said. I looked toward the dust-sheeted bed. "Can I help you make that thing up?"

"The . . . ?" She glanced round, following my eyes. "No. Thank you. I'll do it later."

I groped backward toward the door. "You know——" I began. "You always know——"

She shook her head impatiently and got up from the sill and without looking in my direction moved over to the dressing table. "I'm tired. I'm sick, really sick, physically; and I'm tired. I don't want to know anything, Johnny. *Please!* I want my mind to be a beautiful, perfect blank. I want to be all alone for a while. I just want to be alone. . . ."

I left her. My wife. I found the doorknob and drew it after me and left her. The day that began with a lusty Sarah had now ended with a rejectful wife. I put out the light on my desk in the study and went along to the bedroom Eleanor and I had shared. I took off my clothes and got into bed, but I couldn't sleep. From my grandmother's room still came blurred sounds of movement. I began on fifty authors with four names, but the game was too hard. Authors either have fewer names, or more: Gabrielle Margaret Vere Campbell Long; Esmée Elizabeth Monica de la Pasture Dashwood; Mary Annette Beauchamp von Arnim Russell. Women, of course. And I was goddam sick of women. Ellen Anderson Gholson Glasgow. Well, there was number one, at least.

She'd looked awfully cozy, down there below me in the woods with Ray. Not cozy; no. *Settled.* Comfortably settled. Accommodated according to habit. While he made suggestions that invoked—or placated?—propriety. . . .

Walter Van Tilburg Clark.

But could you count a "Van" as something in itself?

. . . I was falling asleep. From grief, discouragement, and boredom: that most terrible of trios. My most faithful companions. As I lay there, there came to my ears through the open door the faint jingling of chimes. I heard no other sound, but I felt quite sure of what was happening. The pedestal, secure in my nighttime house, was once again on the move.

# 23

I DO not doubt that evil can assume the form of its choosing, but then, it seems to me, evil will choose that form which is most effective for its purpose. Why a pedestal, if mobility is somehow important? And, skewing the question a bit, if mobility is not at issue, why does the pedestal walk?

In the next few days I worried at the problem without reaching either a rational or an irrational conclusion. One trouble was that always, at some point, reason—or, failing that, the sense of comedy—simply balked at the whole business. In spite of what I'd seen, or believed myself to have seen, skepticism intruded. And it was reinforced by the unnatural quiet that now descended on our house. Exhausted by rage, grief, dismay, we slept through the hot, still nights, rose late, and dreamt through the afternoons. My leg improved rapidly, and soon was well. Although Eleanor and I seldom ate together or even occupied the same room except when Sarah was around, there was a comradeship between us. Now and then I actually caught myself feeling at peace, almost feeling happy. We might have been enemies stranded in the same abandoned house in a no-man's-land. The past was useless to us, the future beyond our guessing. Gratefully, amicably, we marked time.

The pedestal, I know now, was doing the same thing—being, in large measure, dependent upon the conditions we created for it. But as it continued quiet I was more and more inclined to regard it as another of those unanswerables that everyone encounters in life. In my maternal grandmother's house a luminous red ball bounced up and down the stairs at night. And her half brother regularly spoke in tongues. My father had a shaving mirror that broke apart the day his younger brother fell through ice and drowned. A great-aunt of mine had all her life the company of a huge dark bird. The family laughed, but in the week she lay in coma, dying, they continued to find ragged feathers dropped down in the hallways, on the stairs; and finally one across her mouth, lifting faintly with her faint half-snore, half-breath. At the moment of her death there was, said her nurse (who, to be honest, enjoyed a good scare), a tremendous vibration in the room like the beating of wings.

Wings. I woke these days to the murmurous plaint of mourning doves in the gutters of the house. I hate their gray sound and the scratch of their discreet, thoughtful housekeeping. On the lawn grackles sat blackly. Once one of those nightmare-big pileated woodpeckers flew heavily out of the woods and landed hard, fat-man awkward, on our drive, sending the grackles up like half-burned leaves in the draft from a bonfire. He waddled in circles, as if hopefully in search of a podium, and then flopped into the air again and dropped back among the trees.

The weather changed. The long dry spell gave way to

violent storms, and the house shook with thunder, the darker rooms and passages flickered with lightning. On a particularly wet, cold, and windy afternoon the Gravatts, at Eleanor's invitation, came for drinks. We had seen them only once since the day following the party, and that was Sunday at church. Alma slipped away before the recessional, and at the door we stopped only briefly to talk to Ray. "You must both come see us soon," Eleanor said, mindful of the congregation pressing behind us or lingering just ahead. I couldn't quite emulate her easy friendliness and merely nodded an endorsement and said something about the sermon. I remembered quite clearly that he'd given it at least twice before, and both times with more flourish and seeming conviction. From finished text it seemed to be going backward to working draft; a pity, since even in its more polished form it had suggested the perfunctory labor of an inattentive mind. But Ray looked ill, standing in the harsh morning sunlight, and I thought perhaps the heat in the church—for this was still in the blazing weather—had been too much for him. He smiled, he touched our hands, and we passed on, down the steps and into the drive. The women all around us were flowers dipping, swaying in their brilliant colors, and where in the crowd there was movement toward friends or toward the family car the effect was of wind running across a garden. That sense of peace overcame me—there had been a particularly beautiful offertory that still sang in my head—and I took Eleanor's arm and after the old habit bumped along at her side. She didn't pull away until we reached the parking lot. But when she did her rejection was unmistakable.

Alma and Ray arrived in a downpour that I think we

were all very thankful for. The first awful minutes were bridged by their dash across our porch, the taking of wet coats, the mopping of faces and smoothing of hair. We were able to be solicitous and they quite gay about the adventure of getting here—which we all knew had involved nothing more than a three-minute drive with a porte-cochere at the start and a covered porch at the finish. But their splendid courage, the ordeal we were agreed they'd been through, made it possible for me to hurry them into the library and press drinks upon them without ceremony, as if only liquor could make up to them for what they'd suffered. All in all, we contrived a commotion that lasted close on fifteen minutes. My own part in this joint effort faltered toward the end—I was glad I had glasses and bottles and ice to attend to. My admiration is wholehearted for people who can carry off situations of this sort with authority, for I am quickly overcome by a sense of unreality. I should rather say, I suppose, that reality itself intrudes too hard. My voice falters in midsentence, and my eyes slip sideways, though not soon enough to miss the eyes slipping in panic away from mine. Horror sets in at the prospect of someone (myself) inadvertently saying the destructively wrong—the hideously true—word. My breath gets short; I suffer from claustrophobia.

Eleanor and I had decided to serve drinks in the library after a good deal of deliberation that had temporarily restored us to one another's company. Alma and Ray were familiars of our living room, the upstairs study, even of our bedroom. In better times we had drunk all over the house. But the library, perhaps because it housed my grandfather's emphatic shade, had formerly been safe from us. It seemed the best solution to the problem of neutral ground—and we were agreed that any place else in the house might swamp us in memories that we couldn't surmount. The barest comment—oh, you've moved that chair; is that a new pillow? it really looks as if that crossandra's going to live, doesn't it?—might recover the intimacy of the past in a way that immobilized us in the present; or, worse, revived the quarrel and put us through still another hell.

I had built a fire, and Alma, drink in hand, was standing on the hearth, shivering a little and looking round at my grandfather's books as if they were a spectacle one rarely had the chance to see. Ray was rubbing the arm of the rocker he sat in, enraptured by the beauty of the wood.

Eleanor said, "We've been sitting in here quite a lot since this weather started. It's so much easier to build a fire than to start the furnace."

Which was untrue on three counts: first, because we weren't sitting together anywhere these days, second, because the furnace had been on since the night before last, and third, because the fire in here was probably one of only a handful that had been lighted since the final time my grandfather came down with a load of books and spent a blissful weekend "weeding" his shelves. I thought suddenly of how well my family seemed to have managed itself, until the generations got to me, and I was struck with shame and envy and with impatience for this absurd, hopeless meeting. I quite forgot that I was in large part its instigator, and wondered if I could last until it was over. Surely, a half hour, forty-five minutes would do? Surely, they would go then? Our only concern was to settle township, parish, county talk, and the Gravatts' simply being here would do that; there was no need to stay the customary cocktail time. In fact, since Eleanor had briefed Sarah the day before—

resolutely ignoring Sarah's astonished mutterings—it had probably been unnecessary for us to go through this ordeal. By now, the amazing news would be all around; no actual meeting was needed for documentation.

I thought of how I would write down particulars of this afternoon later on, on my sheets made from shelving paper, and how it would be night then, and quiet except, perhaps, for thunder breaking on the hills. Like many unhappy people I had come to cherish my solitude, and my life on paper was better at least in the sense that it was less painful. More than that, though: I could make my own order.

Don't say I haven't tried to warn you.

Eleanor and Alma, those mortal enemies, were wonderfully keeping things going, and Ray was coming in now and then with a new parish story that we all found terribly funny and marvelously typical. It really makes me sick to write that, but it says better than any amount of dialogue just how things were in that room, that day. Doctors sometimes suggest a change of scene as an effective form of therapy, but I began to wonder whether even New Zealand would reconcile me to recollections of my Owl Hill neighbors.

When you sit with friends after a critical separation, you cannot help looking at them with a cold eye. I saw how fat Ray was getting in his belly, and how his trouser legs didn't quite meet the tops of his socks. When he turned his head against the fire the fur sprouting from his ears glinted flossy white. He looked shabby in a mail-order way, the cloth of his summer suit fraying and bulging in unlikely places. The corrugated nails on his right hand were all stained gold to pale yellow with nicotine. I had always tolerated his affection for jewelry, but I took a sudden, acute dislike to his familiar ruby-and-gold ring, his wristwatch that was shedding both the leather veneer on its links and its silver plating, and the tiny diamond on his pinky. I could love Alma in any sort of getup, but still I couldn't stop myself regretting her bright, tricky dress, which made one feel that her figure was contained and camouflaged, not opulent but flop. And her makeup, carefully applied, was too thick and colorful: a country conception of glamour that seemed to take its inspiration from the variety-store funny-face.

And what were they making of us? Eleanor had on a white summer wool, very beautiful, very plain. Except for her wedding ring her long, thin hands were naked of jewelry; they beat lightly against each other when she wasn't holding her drink or a cigarette. She wore one of those pale lipsticks that have always struck me as more than a little obscene, and no doubt are intended to produce this impression. In her ears were the tiny emeralds she'd bought herself during her first year at Wellesley; she much preferred them to anything she'd ever received from me. Her hair shone even in that dark room. By chance (since we now dressed separately) I wore white too: white slacks and a pullover sweater with a red line around the neck. We may have seemed like two more among the ghosts haunting this notorious property.

The conversation and laughter gradually became more forced, more extravagant; everyone was wildly searching his memory for *any*thing that might be converted into anecdote, or thrown to the company for impersonal comment. So many topics were taboo that one had first to think through a particular remark before seeming to make a spontaneous offering of it. Would it lead outward into unspeakable areas? Local gossip was of course the main prop of any gathering, but we could hardly at this time pretend a detached amusement for contemporary folklore; that folklore was the reason for our meeting. Which meant that news of the locals was pretty well restricted, too, to things such as somebody's illness or death or marriage, or the birth of a baby. We couldn't discuss the shooting, and even our mutual friends offered difficulties. Eleanor told a small joke about Sybil Fruig's troubles with her new car, and Alma said, "Oh, did she get it? I haven't seen her— It's been ages since we've . . ." And Ray looked grim. I remembered that at our party he'd been furious with Sybil, and perhaps still was. There was a collective relief whenever one of us happened to recall somebody's recent misfortune. We speculated with sympathy on what it would "mean" for the principals—a sympathy that was genuine, but enhanced by our pleasure in feeling not only that other people were bad off also but that here was a topic which with luck we could kick around for ten or fifteen minutes. I noticed that invariably such a potentially useful bit of trouble made everyone lean back and grope automatically for a cigarette.

The electricity failed just as it seemed that the last catastrophe, the last joke, had been thoroughly exploited. God is on the side of one of us, I thought gratefully, getting to my feet. Unless the Gravatts meant to spend the night here, the power failure would carry us through the rest of their visit. In the light from the fire, and what came in through the windows, I found my way out into the hall and over to the massive crystal girandole that stands on a table against the staircase wall. Sarah, fortunately, had put fresh candles in it not long since. We seldom use the girandole, but candles tend to droop very soon in warm weather and also to grow whiskery with a dust impossible to get off. I groped across the table top for a matchbox, nearly stabbing the back of my hand on the sharp point of a dangling luster, and then lighted both wicks and carried the glittering, clinking thing back to the library. To my amusement, I heard Eleanor say, "Dammit, this'll shut off the furnace."

"Ours, too," said Alma, rising and putting her drink on the table beside her chair. "We'd better get back and see whether everything's all right. Oh!" she exclaimed as I put the girandole down. "Isn't that lovely. You ought to light it more often."

"It's in a bad place out there in the hall," Eleanor answered. "Anyone walking past creates a breeze that blows wax around, and then we have a mess. It's terribly hard to clean, too, with all those dingle-dangles that have to be taken off, and I wouldn't want to count the times I've cut myself on that spear thing sticking up in the middle. . . ."

I left them, both so glad of another topic to keep going with, and went down the hall to the closet where I'd hung the raincoats. I was almost there when I noticed that Ray had followed me. "I'm sorry we haven't had that talk yet," he said as I opened the door and groped blindly inside.

"I understand," I said. "Maybe we won't need to now. Things have quieted down." I found his coat and handed it to him. "In some areas," I added.

He patted my arm—a gesture quite unlike him. I didn't know whether I felt more touched or embarrassed. "You're a little up on me, then," he said, and carrying Alma's coat went quickly away.

In the faint light he looked immense but insubstantial. I had suddenly the absurd conviction that we would never meet again.

# 24

Two DAYS later Salmon Willow was arrested for the killing. "He got a fungus in his ear in the war," Sarah said the following morning. "They couldn't get it out, and he's been drinking all these years to ease the pain. It's terrible. He opened an antique shop with his mother's furniture, and before anybody could buy anything he fell over a cord one night and pulled it off the plug and I don't know. The plug was in a socket, and the whole place went up. They hardly got him out. Since then he's been out of work—about twenty years, I guess. He gets some kind of government check that keeps his fungus down."

"Did anyone see him with this girl?" I asked.

Sarah laughed. "Not with her or anybody. He about got down to that beer joint in Oldchurch in the morning, and barely home at night. Joe's found him in ditches, a few times, and hauled him out and took him on to that little shack he has. Oh, my, no! He was a sly one. If you'd of asked me was he drunk all the time I'd said yes. Which isn't to say if he got a woman he couldn't——"

"I follow you," I said hurriedly. "Does he have a car?"

"Never!"

"That girl lived a long way out."

"And too drunk to drive if he did."

"Then doesn't it seem to you that he may be innocent?"

"You forget. The fella doesn't have to drive out; the girl can get *in*."

"That wasn't the way it worked, though. The children, the neighbors have talked about a man being with her."

"Oh, *that* one. I can guess who *he* was. Works in to the liquor store. No, no. Whoever killed her was somebody come and went without nobody noticing especially; or else, like I say, never come much at all."

"Well, I suppose there's a clear line of evidence."

"I don't know about evidence, but he's confessed."

"Confessed!"

"Sure! Walked into the sheriff's office and told them he was their man. He'd been talking about it down at the beer joint for a week or so, but naturally nobody liked to say anything."

"Naturally. . . . So much for the killer being somebody prominent."

"Don't you kid yourself we've heard the end of this. There could be wheels in wheels, if you take my meaning."

"If I don't always take your meaning, Sarah, I have complete trust in your intuition."

"Then I'll tell you something else," she said somberly. "The talk's around that things is going to be very bad for certain people."

"Because of the murder?"

"I couldn't say. But if I was some folks I'd hightail it out of here."

She looked at me so meaningfully that I was driven to a protest. "But I haven't . . . I'm not . . ."

"There's doers and done-to," she answered. "I don't know a thing, except the one's likely to come off as bad as the other. We've never had much, Joe or me either of us, but everybody knows there's a time to cut your losses."

# 25

SALMON WILLOW. He had cold blue eyes, very pale, and a big, lipless mouth without any teeth that you could see, and a tiny, pointed chin. Sometimes when we were out of beer I'd drive over to the Oldchurch joint to buy a six- or eight-pack, and always I'd find Salmon draped or unbudgeably drooped across the bar. He was desperately thin except for a belly that bulged out of him as precisely as if he were a figure in a child's drawing.

The afternoon (only) paper carried a report of his confession, and those wheels in wheels Sarah had talked of began slowly to revolve. Salmon claimed to have been hired for the job, provided with the gun, and issued a map showing him how to find the house. Almost a month ago someone had called him around nine in the morning (an hour before he was due on his stool at the pub) and asked if he were available for work. He'd explained about his fungus and also about his pale blood, his coronary dilations, and his sun cancers. The voice had replied that this particular job required moral rather than physical vigor. Further, it would pay $50 and at the outside would take less than two hours. Salmon, I'd guess, grew more and more eager as his fuddled brain took in the fact that he was being offered good money—$25 an hour, it worked out to—for something that would hardly cut into his busy day at all. His questioners, the paper said, pressed him to find out what kind of work he was so well qualified for that the high rate of payment didn't make him suspicious. The story hinted that Salmon had cited a number of different abilities, but at this point propriety, or the rulings on obscenity, got in the way of detailed reportage. One was left with the vague impression that he had expected to act as middleman in some kind of illicit transaction. Having overheard a fair amount of talk in that Oldchurch bar, I find that propriety is now in my way, too, and that I am content merely to say that any imaginable awfulness probably gets close to what was in Salmon's mind that morning.

The offer of $50 was, of course, very clever; a bigger sum might have awakened his country caution and made him hesitate to meet with his prospective employer. (He said with pride that once he'd found out what he was really being hired for he got the fella up to $180.) Salmon agreed to be at the Oldchurch chapel that evening at ten—a solid indication of his interest, since the bar doesn't close until eleven-forty-five. He was told to enter by the main door, walk slowly down the nave (while counting his footsteps aloud) to the chancel steps, climb these (one-two-three), and turn left into the vestry. There he was to prop himself against the partly boarded rear window but to keep his eyes directed straight ahead into the darkness of the room. His prospective employer would be just outside, and negotiations would be conducted with the crumbling wall between them.

[ 136 ]

It sounds risky—risky for the murderer, that is—but in fact it was quite ingenious and indicated a fairly thorough knowledge of the locality and its people. Like many deconsecrated buildings, the chapel had acquired the reputation of being a dangerous if not downright evil place. I've never heard of lovers in its straggling graveyard, or bums within its doors. And though the vestry is merely a stone shed tacked onto the main building, with its own door to the yard, that door has long since been jammed permanently shut by the weight of the roof slumping down on it. The only way in or out is through the nave. Had Salmon wanted to surprise the other man, he'd have had to go the long way round—by which time his employer would certainly have vanished: over the back wall and into the trees at the side of Miss Wickers' place.

Not that Salmon seems to have had any such idea. The two of them had "quite a nice talk," and found that they "agreed on many things, including United States policy." Here, comedy would threaten to intrude again if it weren't for what came of that and other meetings. What kind of killer begins in such a discursive fashion? What government policy—or policies—were they concerned with? The *who* is almost submerged in the *why* and *what-on-earth*.

At their subsequent meetings—one was two nights later, and the last was some three hours before the shooting—the talk was strictly business. Salmon was reluctant at first because he didn't "know" Mrs. Kinkus. What if he went into the house that according to the map was hers and killed "some innocent person"? That would be "a terrible thing." He was assured that there was no chance of a mistake, since Mrs. Kinkus lived well separated even from her nearest neighbors. "I was worried about her kids, too—how they'd act if they saw me and the hanky on my face fell down," he was quoted as saying. "He told me to do whatever I thought was best, if that happened, but lucky enough I caught her alone, when she was in the kitchen starting to empty garbage. I guess they was all in bed by that time."

So that was that. Salmon claimed to have no idea who he'd been hired by, except it was a man beyond doubt, and the fella had handed over the one-eighty to him like a gent—before he'd done anything, you know, and without seeming to worry about would he just hightail it somewhere. (The Salmon Willows haven't anywhere to hightail it to, which showed again that the killer was someone who knew the town and the township well.)

As to what he felt when the girl turned around from the sink and there he was, pointing a gun at her: naturally he was sorry. She'd looked scared first, and then she'd looked mad, and just before he pulled the trigger she'd looked like she couldn't believe what was happening; almost as if she was going to laugh. He'd hated to do it, almost, even if she'd brought it on herself.

Asked what it was she'd brought on herself, Salmon had looked surprised and said, Well, wasn't she trying to start some trouble? The fella hadn't said too much, but he'd sort of let on that she was out to make whatever mess she could, and if respectable people got hurt that was just too bad. You can't have that kind of thing, can you?

Then, he had killed her without really knowing what threat she posed? Yes and no. She was "dirt." Everybody knew what they were. What they did. You didn't need no blueprint.

As for this ability of his to be "sorry" but resolute: well, he said, he'd been "in the war." The paper added that he appeared surprised when this was not taken as much of an answer. You learned to do what you had to, he went on; and when pressed further said, rather irritably, that it was about like shooting a good hunting bitch that'd started to get in after the neighbor's sheep. A dog that goes bad you got to chain or shoot. Naturally, you can't chain a human being.

I heard later that he seemed honestly puzzled by the horror and contempt his questioners exhibited as he laid out his feelings before them. Finally, after pointing out that he'd come in of his own free will and tried to tell them everything they wanted to know, he withdrew into the proud silence of someone who has done his best though he's had no thanks for it.

And just why *had* he come in? If he'd kept his mouth shut around the bar, and spent his one-eighty discreetly, he'd never have been found out. The question was asked too late: Salmon refused to say anything more. The paper here concluded its first day's coverage—evidently with the notion that this was as good a cliffhanger as any, and that we'd all be scrambling for the next edition with the hope of learning the answer.

In a general sense this was probably true, though I felt sure myself that whatever Salmon eventually said wouldn't really clear up the question to anyone else's satisfaction. He had boasted—at least, he had talked—about the crime in the bar. It was possible that some of his cronies had finally made him turn himself in. Though other crimes were solved in this way, I didn't believe that this was how Salmon's had been. Had anyone put stock in his account?— an old drunk, without a car, without a gun, without a motive (he had prudently said nothing about the money until his interrogation). I could believe that his confession had been a matter of gossip around the village for days, but that the news had been relayed in something of the spirit that I now saw had been at work in the stories about Albert Shardwell's glorious rise to prominence in the case. If you run into the same people every day, you simply have to have something new to talk about with them. Pure invention may serve as well as half-truth, and maybe far better than a bald fact that miserably resists one's best efforts to make it more interesting. Information, after all, is not the prime reason for human exchange; that reason is entertainment.

It remained to be proved, of course, that Salmon, for perverse reasons of his own, was not now entertaining the sheriff's office. The paper indicated, though, that the authorities were satisfied they had their man—or one of them. They'd found the one-eighty (which in itself didn't prove anything, since the bills were well-used and just might have been saved by Salmon over the years). In addition, however, tucked under the money in a coffee can so ancient that the brand was no longer on the market, they'd found the map. It was on onionskin of the kind that is often used for business letter carbons, and traced out the route to the Kinkus house with a care that suggested the killer dealt regularly with very young school children. Every precaution had been taken against misunderstanding or confusion. The paper quoted one notation as, it said, "typical": "Dots show old road. Don't count this as one of 3 you'll pass before turning left into 4th rd."

The notations were printed in ink in block capitals. I wondered how so much information—if all the instructions were as lengthy—had been got on one piece of paper, though the printing was described as "small."

The gun had been "returned." That is, as instructed, Salmon had dropped it through the window of the vestry one moonless night. No, he'd never looked to see whether it had been picked up. Why would he?

The Fruigs came by that evening, and for the several hours while Eleanor and I played man and wife again the four of us talked mostly about the murder and Salmon's confession. Eleanor looked tired and nervous, and several times she tried to turn the conversation to other subjects, but even with assistance from me she had no luck. Bob and Sybil said they were "enchanted" with the map: it was so obviously one piece of evidence that Salmon could never have fabricated—or any of his friends, either. *Imagine* writing out such schoolbookish instructions for a murder!

One doesn't like to differ with friends, or even to let them down in their transports, but Eleanor and I apparently felt the same on the subject: that the horror of the crime made this kind of spirited hashing over both heartless and amoral. Eleanor is usually quite good in difficult circumstances—I could never have managed the ease she brought to our afternoon with Ray and Alma—but I was glad there were some situations she couldn't or wouldn't rise above. Neither of us was rude, or even abrupt; instead, we were awkward, unresponsive, and that struck me as being to our credit.

As they were leaving, Sybil said, "Just the same, you know. It might not be funny."

"It isn't funny at all," I answered. "Any of it."

"No. Of course it isn't. But I was thinking of whoever hired him. Do you remember what we were all laughing about at your party?" She looked at me expectantly. "How it might be one of us?"

"I remember."

"What would we do if it really *were?*"

"I don't suppose we'd do much of anything."

"You sound like Ray. That's what *he* said, and I said, Oh, Ray, that's why we love you. You don't give any moral leadership at all."

"That must have endeared you to him."

She frowned. "We'd have to take *some* kind of stand. And why would I make him mad?" Did she look too hugely innocent? I wondered whether there was more cerebration behind those wide blue eyes than she was generally credited with. Her gaze dropped away from mine, and she added, not quite with her usual style, "Though people are so touchy, aren't they? Sometimes I think I'll drop dead of boredom from having to bother with touchy people."

"Come on, darling," said Bob, putting an arm around her. "I think you're on the edge of dropping dead again."

Sybil pulled away from him. "Johnny? *Johnny* isn't that way. At least, not about the *Gravatts.*" She shot me a quick glance. "Are you, sweetie? That was beautiful of both of you to have them out here, but naturally it didn't fool anybody."

Bob groaned and then took Sybil firmly by the arm and half-shoved her toward the door. "Out," he said. "Out!"

Sybil, leaning backward against him, twisted halfway round and wrinkled her nose in mock disgust. "I'll never marry another lawyer," she declared. "You can't even open your *mouth!* I just said to Ray that he was lucky to be a minister, all things considered."

"What things considered?" asked Eleanor. She'd been silent during this whole unfortunate exchange.

"Ministers don't usually get suspected of things, do they? They're sort of brides of Christ, or something."

"You didn't tell him *that!*"

"I can't remember. But what if I did? Some people ought to be glad of any protection they can get."

"Including Ray?" Eleanor said coldly.

Sybil became evasive. The mischievous smile fled from her mouth and her eyes slid past our faces, out across the lawns. "It can't do him any harm," she answered.

"Let's go, Sybil," said her husband. "I'm not sure what you're hinting at, and I don't want to be. You might keep in mind that Ray's one of my clients."

"Oh, darling, I do! Why else would I really care?" She looked round brightly. "Well! They're bound to get him." Bob groaned. "Whoever it was, I mean," she added, but not hastily. She started down the front steps without any further urging from Bob, and at the door to the car turned round and blew us a kiss. "Don't look so cross. Eleanor, honey. It isn't as if I'd been talking about *Johnny!*"

When they'd driven away, I said, "No wonder Ray's so sore at her. But what weird things to be hinting about him —of all people. He must have said something back to her that's still rankling."

"She's a troublemaker; I've always suspected it. She's delighted to make a crisis. If they ever come here again, you can entertain them yourself."

"You sound as if they were only my friends!"

"They aren't mine."

She went into the library and began to collect glasses. (We seemed to be doing all our entertaining these days in the neutral atmosphere of that room.) I started to follow her, but the set of her shoulders indicated she was thoroughly angry. Why? Because Sybil had gratuitously insulted Ray? Eleanor was not a woman with a disinterested sense of justice, and I couldn't understand why such comparatively harmless malice would rouse more than mild irritation. But I no longer had a secure knowledge of what would please or infuriate her, and to be honest I didn't awfully care as long as she let me alone. We continued generally at peace with one another, but when I ran into her unexpectedly I sometimes found myself caught by the same panic, the same fear, that I'd felt on the first night of our estrangement. Which is to say that my really absorbing preoccupation at this time was with the question of what she had power to do to me. Could she shut me up once more? Could she, at the least, discredit me when I might most need support? Through this long, unnatural spring I had had increasingly a sense of catastrophe approaching, and Eleanor in a way had become its embodiment. There were times when I dreaded the sight of her; she was a darkness falling across my spirit. That I continued to love her filled me with astonishment, and I wondered sometimes whether I was perpetuating this feeling out of an unconscious perversity.

I went upstairs to the desk where my "story" lay hidden under a pile of blank paper in the center drawer. I was working on the sketch of Oldchurch village, but I found I couldn't go on with it; not immediately, at least. My thoughts went back to the murder, to Salmon Willow.

Why *had* he given himself up? I still felt that whatever explanation he came out with would make sense to no one else. He'd wandered into jail as inevitably as he wandered into the Oldchurch bar each night. His fungus had as much turned him into a killer as it had turned him into a drunk. I almost decided that he'd make a blustering statement about "every citizen's duty"—which would confound his auditors, perhaps, but would be absolutely in line with the logic of the Salmons in this place.

I was wrong. My estimate of Salmon was brilliant only in its distance from the mark. He had had a compelling reason for turning himself in.

"I wanted to get here before he did," Salmon said. "I thought he'd tell about everything, and there I'd be. But if I told you first you'd be grateful to me and make it easier."

After this slightly Delphic statement, Salmon was hustled out of the presence of the press (the "press" at this point still being a reporter for the local paper; our broader coverage came later). But it was plain now that, contrary to his earlier story, Salmon either knew or suspected who his employer was. The game was almost up for somebody.

By late afternoon the gossip that it might be "one of us" had been not only revived but magnified. The county rose in speculation: our phone rang repeatedly. I took most of the calls because Eleanor, after talking to a few of our friends, declared she had a headache and was tired of the whole disgusting business. I learned a good deal of surprising information about many of my male neighbors, as did the operators at the telephone company and all of the people who share our supposedly private line. I was astonished at the quantity of profligates in our midst, the former scandals in outwardly convention-ridden families, the number of local marriages on the verge of breaking up. I was not myself proposed as a candidate by any of our callers, but I suppose I figured as handsomely as everyone else in calls to other houses. The county was enraptured: who *was* it? Who on earth was such a *fool?* Even if the girl had talked, the whole business could have been smoothed over. Who was there whom she might have damaged permanently?

What we all found out soon enough took the gaiety from these speculations and left a good many people gray-faced, incredulous. For we were struck in one of our superiorities. That great gong, booming out across the hills, at last stilled almost every voice, and in the interstices of its tremendous, shaking jar there was nothing to be heard except the occasional sound of weeping.

# 26

JUST BEFORE dusk the sky cleared, and we had our first sunset in more than a week. By night the temperature had risen perceptibly, and one or the other of us opened most of the windows in the house. It hadn't really got that warm that fast, but I'd decided to leave the furnace on until I was sure how the weather was settling, and we had both inside and outside heat to contend with. Around eleven I went down to the pool, thinking I'd have a swim if the water was warm enough. It wasn't but I swam anyway. Then I put on one of the thickish robes we keep in the pool house and seated myself beside the bottle I'd brought along. Across the surface of the pool the moon bobbled slowly, and owls barked as if to see it lighted once again. A rabbit screamed somewhere close by, and a train went along through the valley, sounding for a faraway crossing.

I didn't quite get drunk, and I didn't fall all the way asleep; but perhaps I dozed and certainly my thoughts drifted pleasantly, peacefully. I thought of how much happiness I'd found in this place, as a child and then as a man, and I wondered whether my mistake had been to bring Eleanor, an outsider, here. Yet no man can bear himself long alone, and here as elsewhere Eleanor had given me some of my most perfect hours. If I had never quite found out her mind, I had thoroughly found out her body, and until recently this had been enough. The fault was really mine, then, as Eleanor and the doctors all insisted. My euphoria accepted total guilt and passed beyond it to fresh images of pleasure. Perhaps we could never try again with one another—once you have come to be afraid of someone, can that fear ever be dissipated? For her part: once you have rejected your husband as a madman, can you ever again accept a common footing with him? Forbearance, trust require immense reservoirs of understanding and respect, and ours seemed empty. I suppose they had never been anywhere nearly filled.

So my images of pleasure were of the blurred but optimistic kind that leap the muddled present and such practical questions as divorce or legal separation, and ignore the pain of adjustment to a life no longer shared with someone. In effect, each of us was alone already, but the forms we observed, like the ritual of the Church to someone almost lacking in faith, continued to give us a vague reassurance, were still there to lean familiarly back on in our trouble. I decided I might stay on here at Owl Hill for a time. Since neither of us owned the place, it would not be at dispute in whatever disposition of our properties we came to. And Eleanor would be glad enough to get back to our house in Cleveland, whenever she had accomplished the mysterious business that held her here. There was my "story" that I had to finish—or, if not to finish, to set down far enough so that through it I, at least, could come to terms with this time I'd lived. Afterward, I might go ahead with a plan I'd had for years of writing the history of Owl Hill, something that could be privately printed for distribution to the family. My parents, my aunts and uncles, my cousins, my sister, and I all had tales that we cherished among ourselves, even though outsiders probably found most of them of stupefying dullness. Such an activity would especially please my father, who God knew had had little enough joy of his only son. And possibly I'd finish my time at Owl Hill by cataloguing the two libraries: an absorbing, mindless task that would help carry me through the bad period when I finally realized I was getting on for forty and had no wife, no children, no home, no settled existence.

I got out of my chair with middle-aged awkwardness, hugged the robe around me for warmth, and started back toward the house. The moon had ridden the pool and traveled on beyond the trees, and its light guided me up the lawn and the long flight of steps. The heat indoors was tremendously welcome, and for a few minutes I shivered uncontrollably, leaning against the sink and huddling deeper still in the robe until the spasms stopped. When they did, I felt suddenly brighter, as one does after a chill or after a high fever. I decided I'd have a last drink in comfort, and went along toward the living room. I didn't give a thought to the pedestal, and I'd been several minutes in the room before I noticed it was gone.

# 27

Its restlessness was a recurring nightmare, like my quarrels with Eleanor when I thought everything had settled down. Except just now I wasn't so much frightened as irritated. Why tonight? We were no less at peace with one another than was usual of late. The Fruigs? Had they said something to start it up again?

Well, let it walk. I was damned if I'd set out in pursuit, as if its being found elsewhere in the house constituted an indecency. And if Sarah came upon it in the morning, some place it had managed to get into but couldn't get out of, let Eleanor concoct whatever explanation suited her.

Except . . . might this give Eleanor one more weapon against me? Would she just shake her head with a sad bravery and ask Sarah to help her get it back to its place? Eleanor's silence would give Sarah the latitude she could make best use of in carrying the news to our neighbors. There would be no inconvenient facts to be woven into the narrative, or weakly accounted for if she accidentally left one out.

I think now that I was unjust to Eleanor. She had never

intended me to be afraid of her; her plans didn't require fear. And I think, too, of how skillfully she cooperated with me in keeping up the appearance of a normal relationship. That this was useful to her scheme is also true, but I would like to believe that some part of her intention was to be kind to me. Not that it matters one way or the other, any more.

All this is after the fact; on that night I began to be afraid again of what might be done to me, and putting down my drink I started on a thorough exploration of the first floor. At first I moved cautiously, and as quietly as possible, in order to give the pedestal no warning of my approach. Moonlight flooded the rooms on the south and west sides of the house, and there was no need for me to put on lamps or chandeliers in order to search out that unique shape. This was not the case in the eastern rooms, and so I tried to go through all of them swiftly, making no secret of my progress. I found nothing, and only in the music room were there signs such as it might have made in passing: the characteristic half-circular scratches, deeper where it had come down for balance, lighter where it had been in motion. The floor in the music room had just been brilliantly polished, and I could see tracks here and there: but I could make no kind of progression out of them. Had it gone beyond, through the door that opens into the small "office" from which my grandmother ran the house? Had it, instead, come back this way toward the hall?

The scratches might as easily have been made by one of Sarah's cleaning tools. They were simply not clear enough to tell any kind of tale.

Defeated, I went back to the living room, where—need I say?—I found the pedestal in its old place. The cold moon picked out its elaborate flank, the top that continued to suggest to me a ruff without a head inside. It seemed scarcely aware of me, abstracted; so much at ease in my presence that it didn't need to give me its attention whenever I came upon it. We saw one another too often, were too closely involved, to make that kind of thing any longer necessary. Whatever it had been up to tonight, playing a game with me had been no part of its purpose.

I remembered thinking once that the pedestal and I were yoked in a momentous conspiracy—yet, as in my human relationships, I was left uninformed about the issues that moved us, the dangers we faced; the danger we were. Was this my madness? But hadn't Sarah given me warning of terrible things to come? of the wisdom of flight? Or had I understood her to fit not the reality she suspected but my own increasingly vivid apprehensions?

There was only one thing, just then, that I was sure about: that the pedestal must be stopped. We wouldn't wait for the child of inspiration to tell us how to cap it. For the present, at least, anything that rode skiddingly, that would fall with a crash, would make it difficult for the pedestal to move without giving itself away.

I went back to the hall and got the girandole from the table beside the stairs, almost stabbing my palm, in the dark, on that dangerous finial that Eleanor had remarked to Alma about. Rising some twelve inches above the center of the piece, it is at once its principal adornment—a crystal obelisk sharp as a spear—and greatest hazard. Carefully and slowly —because the lusters fall off at the least opportunity—I walked the length of the living room and slid the girandole's square, padded base onto the pedestal's top. The lusters swung and sang against the moon. I stepped back, and I thought I saw the whole mass move just slightly, with affront or surprise. I am not sure, but it is a fact the lusters sang more loudly for a time, more brazenly and harshly, calling down the moon among them to dance with manic gaiety.

# 28

I NEVER finished my drink. I suppose Sarah either emptied or downed it the next morning. Almost staggering with sleepiness, I went straight to bed, thankful I had only to get out of the sandals and drop the robe on the floor before tumbling in. My clothes were in the pool house, and if it rained during the night they'd be safe.

On the edge of sleep I thought comfortably that should the pedestal now choose to move I would in a sense be free of it. That is, no one could dispute its peculiar powers, for mine would no longer be a solitary faith. Then, as I rode gently on the first wave of oblivion, the mistake I'd made brought me sharply awake. The pedestal would first have to be seen, supporting that child not of inspiration but of despair. If the pedestal walked before morning, and the girandole was discovered a rainbow glitter round its base, my strategy would fail. I could imagine Eleanor's anger, Sarah's relish for the strange things I did at night. Carrying that there clinky thing around in the dark. Whyever for? a person'd wonder. Well, he don't have much to say for hisself, and my idea is he don't know no more than we do.

Drunk, I guess. Him and Salmon Willow'd make a pair. He went prancing around with it, and then I guess he took a header over something, and down it went. Lucky he didn't get cut to pieces—drunk's luck.

I groaned out loud, from rage and frustration, but I was too tired to go downstairs and put the girandole back in its old place until morning. The hell with it, the hell with the pedestal, the hell with Eleanor, Sarah . . . everybody. If the girandole got smashed, I'd put a lamp up there, or the bust of Dante in the cellar; as fast as one thing was broken I'd stick up another until finally, finally somebody took the point. And in the meantime I'd swear up and down that all this breakage was as much a surprise to me as to anyone else. Let them try to prove otherwise. . . .

I woke late the next morning, to blazing heat and the promise of worse to come, and to the news that Ray had been found dead, head under and belly sticking out, in a tub in one of the rectory bathrooms.

# 29

ELEANOR TOLD me; she was just putting the phone back when I came down. I was too shocked to think of asking who'd called. On Eleanor's face every line showed; she looked as if she'd been stitched together with invisible thread. One hand went halfway out toward me and then—I was not too numb to notice—drew back, closed round her other wrist.

"When?" I asked finally.

"Last night sometime. At least, that's when he usually took a bath. Though she didn't find him until an hour ago, so they don't really know yet. He left a note. That's what they say, anyway. It wasn't for her. It was just . . . a note, for anybody who . . . found him."

A note? A *note!* "My God, I thought it was an accident!" I was too overcome by the fact of Ray's death to react much further, and even my thoughts were slow to reorder themselves. Finally, it occurred to me to say, "He must have tried to explain; he must have wanted Alma—somebody, anyway—to know why he did it."

Eleanor shook her head, rather as if to clear it than in

any response to me. "Who can't guess why he did it?" she said. Her hands dropped to the telephone in its cradle, and she hunched forward above it. "Oh, the *fool!* The absolute *fool!*"

"I can't guess," I told her.

She looked up at me with contempt. "Because of Salmon Willow, of course. In heaven's name, who did you think Salmon was talking about?"

# 30

I GROPED for the newel post behind me, backed round it, and sat on a step, incapable of answering her. I'd known Ray off and on for years, whenever we'd come down here or when I'd run into him at a diocesan convention; and since we'd settled in at Owl Hill we'd been—until recently, at least—as close as perhaps any priest can be to members of his own parish. There are those final reserves that a priest must invoke or lose something of his efficacy. But many reserves can be peeled away before these ultimate ones are reached, and Ray and I had had some intimate talks on various occasions. I don't mean that I was surprised he'd never mentioned the hill girl, the tragic Mrs. Kinkus with her awful name. Rather, I wondered that I'd never sensed, either by what he said or what he left unsaid, by attitude or glance, that he was or could be involved in this kind of situation. The old saw about watching out for the quiet ones isn't very accurate. Was Mrs. Kinkus Ray's first, or simply because of circumstances his last?

I said, "We've got to go to Alma."

Eleanor straightened herself and wrapped her arms tightly around her waist. Despite the heat, she was shivering violently. "Oh, Alma! Alma, forever and forever."

"Did she know?"

"I suppose so. She must have been suspicious, at least."

"Yet, neither of you said anything."

"Would you have?"

"I think I would. Yes."

Eleanor came round the newel post to where she could look at me directly. "If *I'd* killed—I don't know: some man I'd got involved with?"

"Murder settles nothing."

"You would have?"

"Yes."

"You really aren't human," she said venomously. "You're insane. You're worse than the worst I ever imagined you were."

"Afterward, I'd have done everything I could to help you."

"Help! What good would help be to me then? What would *help* settle?"

"All right. Forget it. It's a hypothetical question."

"At the moment. If I change my mind I'll know who to start with."

"That girl . . . Did you know about her when it was going on?"

"How else do you suppose I guessed he'd done it? You can't really believe he ever took me aside and confessed!"

"I suppose not. No. But . . . how did you find out about them, to begin with?"

"I made it my business to."

"Why?"

"That's no concern of yours any longer." Eleanor turned away and went down the hall toward the dining-room door. "I *had* to know. She could have been part of my plans."

# 31

I GOT up and started swiftly after her, meaning to ask what the devil she was talking about, what she was implying. But the floor polisher started just as she disappeared beyond the door, and when I followed I came on Sarah, working away industriously and looking grave, happy, thoughtful, as so many people do when they find themselves close to a tragedy or scandal that has no personal effect on them. I was confident she'd heard the better part of our conversation and I was damned if I'd provide any further entertainment. Eleanor had gone through the swinging door into the butler's pantry, and I turned back, finally coming to indecisive rest beside the telephone.

So much was becoming clear to me: Ray's uneasiness, his fear, as I saw now, at my references to the hill girl when he and I had talked in my grandmother's room during the party. The way Alma had got up abruptly and left when Sybil came over to ask what we were discussing. *"One of us what?"* *"One of us did the shooting."* Alma's attempt, later in the television room, to reduce the subject to something requiring only a conventional response: *"Yes, it was*

*terrible. . . . We've all been shocked.*" And, of course,
Eleanor's constraint yesterday when the Fruigs got going
on the murder. I'd been my usual foolish self, believing that
on this one subject, at least, our sensibilities were in accord.

How had she risked meeting him alone in the woods?
Had she felt no danger? Surely, she knew that he, with a
killer's heightened perception, would guess her knowledge.
It appeared now that he was a one-time killer, a man in-
hibited from further action by either conscience or fear. I
remembered that Salmon Willow judged him so, too. But
could Eleanor have been so sure of him, that much time
ago, unless there existed between them a relationship which
nothing could alter? No, no. I wouldn't dwell on that now.
I wouldn't, I wouldn't. . . . My first job was to see Alma,
to find out how I could help her, comfort her; what there
was that she still might be protected from. Yet, I couldn't
go to her if she was alone, and clearly Eleanor had no intention of coming with me.

I called Bob Fruig at his office, and his secretary, in the
hushed voice of an usher at a church funeral, told me that
Mr. Fruig had been "called away quite suddenly." In my
agitation I misheard her and thought for an incredulous
moment that Bob too was dead. When I'd got myself under
control I asked whether Mr. Fruig was by any chance at
the Gravatt residence (it is curious how a house becomes a
residence in solemn hours)? The secretary, a Mrs. McCaskie
whom I know quite well, asked whether I would be Mr.
Bayden. When I assured her I would be, she dropped her
voice almost to the point of inaudibility and said that it was
her "understanding" that Mr. Fruig was "on his way."
Then, once more becoming my old friend, she told me
how they were all "at sixes and sevens here. Just so

*shocked!*" I applauded and allied myself with their sensibility and hung up. The best plan I could think of was to drive past the rectory and see whether Bob's car was parked outside. If it wasn't—and I saw no other familiar car—I'd go on to Oldchurch, turn round, and try again. Since another person's tragedy affords so many people a sense of duty, importance, and solemn glee, I suspected that the rectory drive would in fact be swarming with cars. If so, of course, there was no real reason for going myself at this time. But because of the scandal of a probable suicide and the stories traveling round about Alma, there was the off-chance that she just might be alone, except for Bob. The thought was unbearable.

I went upstairs and changed to dark trousers and white shirt, and as an uncertain afterthought collected a gray wash-jacket and slung it over my shoulder. At the foot of the stairs I met Sarah, and my heart sank before that bird of malediction with its shining eyes.

What she had to say, though, surprised me, for it took me back to a matter that now seemed to belong in some other man's past.

"Mr. Bayden!" she said. "Who stuck that thing on top of it?"

The riddle of the pronouns again; another time, she might almost have made me feel nostalgic about happier and better days at Owl Hill when she and her stories and her pronouns were among our liveliest interests.

"The girandole?" I asked, and got a blank look. "The big candleholder on the pedestal, you mean?"

She nodded. "That one that's always set on the table here."

"I put it there."

She raised her hands in thanksgiving. "I was afraid . . ." she began, and laughed. "I wondered was it starting to collect things on its own." She stepped aside. "I don't want to hold you up. You got your sad job to do. It looks real nice there."

"I thought we might try out various pieces."

"Looks to me like you got it the first time. My, it does dazzle! That come from a good store, I bet."

"My great-grandmother owned it. I don't know where she brought it from."

"Well, it come from a good store to start with, you can be sure of that. Today's my day to oil the blamed thing again, which is how I noticed. I certainly hope the poor soul's bearing up."

There were several lightning shifts of subject here, but I had no trouble keeping abreast of them. "Nobody really bears up, Sarah. The best anybody manages is to keep going somehow."

"She's got her old auntie with her. I guess that'll help."

I'd been just about to open the front door and leave, since it's hard to terminate a conversation with Sarah gracefully. She couldn't have stopped me more effectively with a bullet.

"Miss Brainton?" I asked incredulously.

"Miss Dorothy Violet Brainton."

"But they . . . " I was too startled to be circumspect. "Do they know each other?"

Sarah launched into one of her inimitable cackles and then, remembering the gravity of the situation, cut it off sharply. "I guess they ought to. Old Dorothy's there once a week to supper, and Mrs. Gravatt she does the shopping for her at Ned's whenever arthritis don't let her out. The poor soul's helpless as a June bug on its back, a lot of the time, you know."

"I didn't—it's all news to me." And then, as I groped for a further observation, something struck me. "You knew about . . . You'd heard of Mr. Gravatt's death before you came this morning?"

"Why, sure!" She looked at me with an amused tolerance that she saw no reason to conceal. "Hardy Ethrop down the road's been on the Gravatts' private line for years. He heard the missus tell the doctor when he picked his phone up to call the Co-op. Fact is, Hardy's the one told old Dorothy, and she got him to come fetch her right off."

"I see." I could think of no suitable response to this remarkable, this typical explanation, and said stupidly, "This is a time when family should rally round." After which I made a hurried exit.

As the screened door shut behind me I heard Sarah's cackle again, and her parting remark: "Ain't that for sure!"

Miss Brainton. I'd seen her only twice, rolling hugely down the street in her sturdy saddle shoes, her sticklike legs vanishing upward under pleated skirts of brilliant color and design. She had a mop of blonde hair and a face that was feverish with rouge and lipstick. She lived up beyond Miss Wickers, the third or fourth house above the chapel: a shanty place with brown asphalt brick veneer and a metal chimney that leaned out across the roof. It had two front doors, side by side, and I'd been told that they opened into the same room. One was the weekday door, one for Sundays; some sort of religious requirement. You see these double doors all over the northeastern part of the state, but the faith they represent—or that some of them represent—seems to have come south only as far as the Brainton household.

If I was surprised to learn of the Gravatts' association with Miss Brainton, I nevertheless thought better of them for having made a regular effort to entertain her and to help her when she was ill. Yet the open connection had probably done Alma more damage than good in the village view. When had it begun? I thought it couldn't be long-standing, simply because it was only recently that talk of the relationship had begun to go round. As long as Miss Brainton kept her mouth shut, it would have been easy for Alma to visit her under the pretext that she was calling on a needy golden-ager. Certainly there were any number of those in the area, and St. Peter's had never made any distinction between communicants and other residents. But somehow word had got out: Miss Brainton had said something, or Alma had: I hoped that Alma had grown weary of duplicity and decided to outface public opinion. Surely that would be more characteristic than that she found herself trapped into acknowledgment by her own or another's indiscretion?

Well, whatever the truth, she was paying dearly for the relationship: I didn't doubt that the wicked, unanswerable gossip about her had originated in recollections of the Brainton family's past. And while Alma stood convicted of vague but unspeakable conduct, Ray had pursued the affair with the hill girl. And with others?—with at least one other? I fought clear of terrible suspicion still again. There was no way at the moment to deal with it, and to let it take obsessive hold of my brain, my emotions would be merely to deepen my sense of loss and shock and betrayal.

The heat seemed worse than what we'd had before the

rains and cold weather. I felt lightheaded and realized I'd had no breakfast, not even a cup of coffee. And I had the makings of a first-class headache. Below me, the roof of the garages shimmered with sunlight. A hummingbird was spearing the lantana that was beginning to bloom in a bed beside the drive. Just beyond, bees circled above their ground nest near the base of a dogwood. I was reminded of the mud daubers' hut under the front porch roof that would soon have to be smoked out if we weren't to abandon that part of the house altogether.

In fact, a number of small jobs came to mind that suddenly seemed imperative. I found that I was loitering down the drive, undecided about which was the most immediately attractive: the Venetian bench that needed to be taken all the way apart and then glued back together, the clogged-up cellar drain I'd borrowed a metal snake to poke through, the gutters that should be cleaned out where the screening had rusted away . . . Not to mention the asparagus beds that had better be salted before they vanished in weeds, or the kindling I kept chopped up well ahead, even though the gas cradles in the various fireplaces made kindling less than entirely necessary. . . .

Well, what was there for me to do for Alma right now? —except to remind her, by my presence, of other shames, other miseries. Was it only momentum that kept me going? Wouldn't I do better to call later, tonight or tomorrow? With Miss Brainton in temporary residence, there'd be no risk of a seeming impropriety, even if I turned up when other visitors had gone.

This was rationalization, plain and simple; I knew it even at the time. Nevertheless, my descent of the drive got slower and slower. Finally, I turned off onto the lawn and went down a slope to the concrete steps that lead down through boxwood to the rear door of the pool house. For reasons good, bad, or mixed, I meant to delay my visit. Maybe the truth is that I was suffering from the lassitude, both moral and physical, that sometimes follows shock, especially when shock has been preceded by a long period of growing stress. Or maybe, like a child, I was invoking symptoms and reasons merely to get myself clear of the whole business.

I felt an overwhelming desire for sleep, and in the pool house, already blinking, yawning in the half-dark, I picked up an air mattress and took it out into the sun. Then I threw down my coat, stripped off my shirt, and stretched out face downward. I was asleep almost at once, and I slept so deeply that when at last I woke it was with a sense of blissful estrangement from the complexities of the present. I still belonged, however briefly, to that comprehensive, supportive dark, and I felt a physical well-being such as I hadn't known in days.

A hand on my shoulder was what roused me, and a voice saying, "Mr. Bayden! Mr. Bayden!" Sarah, kneeling above me on the corner of the mattress. "Mr. Bayden, you'll be burned to a crisp you stay out in this much longer. I can see red under the brown already."

I brought her slowly into focus; more slowly still I took her warning in. Then I moved, and the skin across my back resisted somewhat, as if it were paper lightly glued in place. "Thanks, Sarah." I sat up and rubbed my eyes.

"I come down to vacuum out the pool, is how I found you," she explained. "You ought to put something on there."

"Yes. I will. I'm still waking up. What time is it?"

"It's past one. I was listening to the news while I washed up my lunch dishes, and that goes off five after."

"Was there any more about . . . us?"

"Nothing new, but they sure were going over everything us out this way knew already."

"I didn't get far with my sad duty, as you can see."

"Time enough later," she said comfortably. "I'll bring that jar out of the pool house."

"No, don't bother. We've got some prescription stuff up in our bathroom, and it's much better. Has Mrs. Bayden had lunch, too?"

"You couldn't prove it by me. She's long gone."

"Gone?"

"Soon after she thought you'd left. Off to the doctor again, I guess."

Her eyes danced and glittered and fixed me with amusement, curiosity, tenderness: what was it they were piercing with?

"Doctor . . . ?"

"Well, Camp, isn't it? He's the usual one all you folks go to."

Dr. Camp, Edwin B. Camp, 229½ Oldchurch Road.

Edwin B. Camp, Obstetrician. He was indeed the one all us folks went to during pregnancies.

"Yes," I said. "Yes, of course."

"I only found out the other day," said Sarah. "My sister seen her coming out of his office. You're a pair of sly ones."

"Well . . ."

"I understand. All these years, and then suddenly . . . You feel kind of sheepish at first, and don't exactly want to talk about it, no matter how glad you may be. Oh, I understand."

I looked at her, quickly; then away. And she did understand, but nothing she'd given words to. She flashed, simpered, shot me glances meant to yield up whatever interpretation I chose to put on them. She was subtle, brilliant; cruel without wishing me any more suffering than she would need in order to carry home a good story—something to compensate for her hard day, her mean life.

"Yes," I said; "sheepish. And . . . surprised, of course."

"Who wouldn't be! I guess your folks were?"

"We—that is, I . . . I don't think they know yet. Any of them. They'll be . . ."

"Won't they, though? Won't they just ever!"

I got quickly, clumsily to my feet. She had enough of my misery to feed on; I'd give her no more. "I'd better get up to the house and put something on my back."

"You look after yourself. You both got a few more months before you shouldn't, from the look of her, and no sense wasting them." Sarah choked on her own ribaldry.

"No sense," I agreed, fleeing. "None at all."

A baby, a baby, I thought, flying upward, taking the kitchen steps two at a time. Mine? Oh, surely mine, the child we'd wanted so badly. Hadn't we? Wouldn't we, even now? I didn't know what Ray's role was. Had been. But I was the father. Oh, God, surely I was the father.

I came through the kitchen door with the speed of a man going somewhere besides a medicine cabinet. But she wasn't there for me to seize, to hold, to cry with in deep joy. I was alone in the vast house I had always so much loved and Eleanor had not quite, ever, come to terms with. I moved toward the front stairs, through the butler's pantry, the dining room.

When could she have told me, really? That is, what good

[ 170 ]

occasion had we shared lately? There had been none. Since that truly happy day of the auction and the trip back through the hills, the pedestal lolling in the seat behind us, we had known no peace, and there had been little enough joy between us.

Was this the news she'd confided to Ray? And had she told him for lack of anyone else to tell it to? I remembered, at our party, his saying that she talked to him. He had asked me what better person she could choose. And if they wanted to meet on a hillside, under trees . . . There is no greater privacy than your own grounds afford, and if you are noticed who has a better right to the place? And, also, perhaps Eleanor found it easier to speak candidly in such a setting.

Except . . .

*What* had she wanted to convey to him? Her joy, her distress? It struck me suddenly, plainly, that Eleanor was always candid with intention. Supposing I'd guessed her confidence correctly, the next question was where it was meant to lead.

I had come by now into the entrance hall. And there I heard the music of the lusters on the girandole. I hovered, foot-silent, but the thin, frail sound did not get louder. The pedestal only shuddered, tentative, trying its keeper out.

The pedestal, too, or so it seemed to me then, had its further intention; some dreadful end that it worked toward.

# 32

AFTER ALL, I did go to see Alma, but less from concern, affection, than from a restlessness I couldn't control. It set in as the pain of my back was subsiding. Utterly distracted, no small distractions could sustain me across whatever time separated this moment from that of Eleanor's return. I couldn't write. My various domestic projects required too much of either thought or effort. I went to the rectory because it was the only possibility still open to me.

I encountered there, in the person of Alma, a woman transfigured by her loss. Beautiful, desirable to me always, she was now resplendent. It is, of course, a phenomenon of loss through death, at least where women are concerned, but I had never before observed so much magnificence. She bloomed, gleamed, was all softness and lovely colors; perfectly composed, and generous in her sympathy—so I noticed within minutes of my arrival—for those who had summoned the courage to come and see her. It was soon apparent that the probability of Ray's having killed himself was generally known, but I was fairly sure, after listening in on a half-dozen casual exchanges, that his motive was not common knowledge. The usual assumption was an unspecified illness that of course was taken to be cancer. Alma, in my hearing, did not offer contradiction.

If this were a well-managed narrative, I should have to make some kind of report on Alma's aunt. The truth is, however, that I didn't see her and have no idea where she was. Gone home again, possibly. Shall I invent an occasion for my manuscript? Shall I put a face on her, give her words portentous or flatly declarative? I could have her say, as I bent above her murmuring condolence, "And you have lost your wife, I understand?"—an old woman's confusion over gossip only half-understood or badly reported.

—Wait, though. Isn't *this* my narrative? Or do I conceive of still another, a kind of reflection with, beyond it, still another, and one beyond that?—a succession, each subtly distorting, forcing the eye to choose for itself the ultimate image. And that, perhaps, is entirely different: a totally created thing.

I began so simply. Where have I carried myself?—and Eleanor, and the others in these pages?

The image I shall choose for myself will contain a truth somewhat truer than experience but less than that of the dancing, articulate imagination. So I decide at this moment, anyway. Trust me this far only, then; beyond, you must settle matters for yourself.

It was impossible to get Alma alone in the crowd at the front of the house, and seeing her slip through a door I followed her to the kitchen, thinking I might fare better there. But here were more crowds: women from the parish making coffee and sandwiches. The atmosphere was festive, for death brings out not only what is most generous in people but what is most spontaneously gay, joyous. The women tried for solemnity when we came in, but the attempt was halfhearted, soon abandoned.

Sybil Fruig was one of the group, and since she saw me at once I felt I had to go over and speak to her. She was, for Sybil, and among these women, unusually subdued.

"Well, Johnny?"

"Hello, love. Is Bob still here?"

"No. He had to be in court. Then he was going back to the office." She looked quickly around and dropped her voice. "He's afraid the real news will break before the day's out, and then we're going to have reporters coming in from everywhere." Her eyes narrowed. "You know what I'm talking about?" I nodded. "Well," she went on, "as Alma's legal representative he's hoping to draw some of the mob off. Of course it will be only a delaying action, but it'll give Alma that much more time. He's sure we're to be very big news before this is over. Scandal in Eden—we'll all be involved."

"What if we got Alma out of here? Wouldn't that help, too? She could come back with me."

"Oh," Sybil said, "with *you!* For what?—fifteen seconds, until Eleanor spotted her?"

"Eleanor wouldn't——"

"Eleanor would. Look, Johnny, we all like you and we've really gone out of our way. But it hasn't worked. She doesn't like us, and we . . . Well—" Sybil hunched her shoulders—"the thing is that this is no time to be testing an imaginary good will."

It was no time, either, to speculate on the extent of the hostility toward Eleanor that until today had been covert.

Sarah first; now Sybil. Both of them women I had often found in animated conversation with my wife: smiles, gestures, lowered voices.

I said, "All right. I won't press it. But surely somebody else here could take Alma?"

"Yes, certainly, if she'll go. She's . . . I suppose I needn't tell you how she is?"

"I can see that for myself. She's remarkable."

"All of that! Yes. But I meant—not something more than you mean, but perhaps something to one side." Sybil looked at me with that intelligence I'd begun to suspect her of only recently. "Alma is a woman who holds onto her unhappiness. She loves it and keeps it warm and blooming. Ray has been her great support all these years. He never let her down; he always fed her misery. Now that he's dead she'll need to find her suffering somewhere else. So I think we'll none of us persuade her into hiding, you see. She'll want to be right at the front. She may"—Sybil smiled faintly—"be furious with Bob for whatever he manages to spare her."

"I can't believe you," I said. "It's terrible. You do her a terrible injustice."

Sybil put her hand on my arm. "I shouldn't have told you. I know—everybody knows—how you feel about her. It doesn't mean she isn't *good*, Johnny; it's the way she is. Don't you know anything about Ray? Has so much been kept from you? She couldn't have put up with him all these years if she were otherwise."

"I want to talk to her," I said, not meeting Sybil's eyes, not yet wishing to take in what she'd told me.

"Yes, go talk to her. She's gone out on the back porch. Maybe she's alone. . . . Poor Johnny!"

I glanced back toward her before I went outside. She stood, a jar of sandwich spread in one hand, watching me with so much pity and distress on her face that I felt, quite terribly, as if the principal loss on this day, the greatest grief, was mine.

# 33

ALMA WAS not on the porch, and at first she seemed to have disappeared completely. Then, barely in time, I saw her on the last step leading up to the door in the west transept of the church. She pushed the door open and walked slowly inside.

I almost went around the house and back to my car. But suddenly I felt—though without any good reason—that we might never again have a time to talk in. And so I followed her, intending to go quietly away if she looked to be in prayer. I remembered the Sunday morning when the pretty women had seemed like flowers, and for the time it took us to reach the parking lot Eleanor and I were man and wife again. That seemed to me an interlude of purest joy; I suppose because I forgot briefly that we'd been dissembling then, too. Or because dissemblance thereafter was so much more difficult, empty of hope.

What a day this was, intensely hot, the sun creating a white immensity that held, in its sheer emptiness, a sort of trembling terror. The landscape shifted minutely; the glare flickered; one thought there were distant explosions, commotions, almost but not quite heard. With effort I kept myself from lifting feet high to meet an undulating foreground. I pushed open the swinging door to the transept and stepped into the tiny, windowless vestibule, and had to stop there, blinded, the darkness swimming. Then I groped on, found the second door into the church proper, and quietly—I might almost say stealthily—turned the knob.

Light sprang at me; the interior seemed brilliantly supported, contained by it. Erect, motionless, Alma stood close to the baptismal font at one side of the chancel steps, her shadow blackly across the marble basin. To her left, but closer to me, a great gold cross burned with splendor above the islanded sanctuary.

I went quickly toward her, while my nerve held, and more silently than was my intention—for she whirled half round, her face gone white, a nerve at one corner of her mouth twitching, her put-out hand defensive, shaking. I took it in both of mine, but I was unable to speak: the comforter needing comfort, the mourner dry-eyed. So we stood, a little absurdly, her features once again composed, almost compassionate, and mine wrinkling with a sorrow I couldn't express, hadn't until this moment even felt.

"I came," I managed finally to say. "That's about all there is to it."

"That's all there needs to be," she answered, withdrawing her hand, though not unkindly.

"But I haven't come generously, as I wanted to—as I meant to."

"Generously?"

"In the most concerned spirit. I started for here this morning, and I didn't get as far as the garage. Now I'm here because there's nothing else I feel able to settle to."

She turned somewhat away from me and murmured, vaguely, "You mustn't tell me this."

"I must! It's the best generosity I can offer you. We've hung on, you and I, haven't we?—not successfully, but at least we've kept something."

Alma shook her head. "No, we've kept nothing. There was so little; you must see that now. Ray and I, you and Eleanor, the four of us . . ."

"But you and I . . . !"

"Let me return your generosity. Don't ask me to answer."

"No. The three of you have shut me out of everything long enough. Your only generosity toward me can be the truth."

"My poor Johnny, you make me tell you: you were what I had to turn to, to distract me from my hopelessness. Does Eleanor hate me because she's jealous—or because she guessed my insincerity? It was such a relief, the little thing we had, because you knew nothing, suspected nothing. Ray said—you must take this as my most generous gift to you—that you had the purity and innocence of madness. You were uncorrupted by what was happening around you. Yours was the sheltered life in the best beauty it can have for people like us."

Ray had said something of the same sort to me, once. But her words broke me as his had not; much as she had done a moment earlier, I said, "Don't tell me anything more."

"I must, having started; we've got to finish up, wherever that carries us." She added, nervously, rapidly, "I'm glad you forced this. If we're to go on, either of us, we'd better understand our terrible condition."

"You knew what Ray had done?"

"I kept turning my mind away from the possibility. Always, before, he'd broken with them so amicably. Why should it have been different this time? If I'd had any knowledge of the drift of things . . ."

"There's no use——" I began conventionally.

"——blaming myself? I don't. Nothing I might have done would have saved her. It was in the note, you see: *she* broke with *him!* He wasn't ready—and he had a murderous vanity. People will say they'd reached some sort of crisis, that she was threatening exposure, and I'd rather they'd say that, much rather. But what chance, really, would she have had against his power, his prestige? She struck him where he *was* vulnerable: the poor, silly thing lost interest in him—I suppose wanted to take up with someone else. He would never have stood rejection from a girl of her sort."

As I had with Sybil, I cried, "It's terrible, terrible!"

"He was terrible," Alma said quite simply. "But for some women he was fascinating, engrossing. They pored over him. I understood them; I pitied them. I'd begun that way myself."

At last, in the easiest manner, I was able to bring up my wife. The question I'd dreaded to look at directly, and dreaded more to get an answer to, came out as if our whole exchange had been leading toward it. I said, "Was Eleanor one of them?"

Alma looked first surprised, then considering and, for what reason I didn't then understand, rather sad. "No. Never, I think; certainly not since you've been at Owl Hill this time. I'd have known."

"Then why were they meeting?"

"Were they?"

"Down in our woods. I saw them. They were talking as

people do who . . ." But I couldn't finish, not because of pain or embarrassment or distress but because I was less and less sure how they had talked. Perhaps it was this uncertainty, growing in me without my awareness, that had finally made the question easy. My dread had diminished.

But Alma's silence was so prolonged that dread began to return, and a panic that set small flashes running through my wrists and cut off my air supply as effectively as if someone had pushed a blanket down over my nose and mouth.

Her hand closed firmly on mine. "You must bear this," she said. "As I've borne my rejection." She went on quickly, perhaps for my sake, perhaps for her own. "Eleanor wanted to lose the baby. She couldn't ask her doctor to name someone, so she turned to her priest—her profane, ingenious priest." I must have started, shown in the midst of shock and rage my simple surprise. "But of course!" Alma exclaimed. "Who knows more about the resources of a community than a minister? He could have sent her to three or four, I suppose. And she begged him; he told me how she pleaded with him. Because of your illness, what it had done to your marriage, she hated the child—the thought of it, the thought of you."

I began to tremble, and looking at me Alma must have guessed the extent of my innocence. I said, "Her jealousy . . . the scenes she went on making. . . ."

"She couldn't quite let you go; not just yet."

"She should have left me."

"I think she will now. She'd never have gone as long as there was hope of bringing Ray around."

"Why didn't he tell her someone to go to?"

"Scruple?" Alma lifted her brows as if to admit the hopelessness of inquiry. "All we can be sure of is that he held fast; he finally forced her to see Dr. Camp, for her own sake if not for the child's."

"Camp's knowing would make it difficult to lose the baby without rousing suspicion."

"Oh—" Alma shrugged—"difficult; not impossible."

"She'd found out about the girl; she guessed the rest. I think she meant to threaten him, if she finally felt he wouldn't give in to her."

"Perhaps she had already."

And driven him to kill himself?

Alma must have guessed the way my mind was working, for she shook her head and said, "No, he condemned himself; not even the danger from Salmon Willow influenced him very much. After all, he was a man who had had a vocation once."

I felt that neither of us could bear much more. Lowering my head, beginning to turn away, I said, "And you?"

"Everything will come out. I'll go away as soon as they'll let me. The Bishop's being very kind. He called late this morning, and he'll be down tonight. This is terrible for him, too, for the Church. And there is the problem of the funeral: suicide and . . . the fact of another death also being involved. . . ."

She fell silent, and for a time we stood together in the glowing light. Above the sanctuary the great gold cross flashed and dimmed. Then, without speaking again, Alma drifted away from me, back into the west transept, toward the door opening onto the lawn between the church and the house. The darkness of the vestibule accepted her; she was gone.

# 34

THE HARDEST, the cruelest thing about grief, about loss, is that you think somehow if you manage to survive at all you'll live through it by weathering through it; day by day the load will get less terrible to endure. That's what you think. And then you begin to get better, to stretch yourself a little, move with a small freedom, and the thing hits you again, as bad as it was at first. The agony is almost worse because you know suddenly that what has filled up your hours of loss has been the company of the sense of loss itself. Now you're bleakly alone, so alone that only death itself, the possibility, that is, of your own dying, is strong enough to offer consolation.

I went home, out the rectory drive and into that familiar road. On either side of Maryella's Run the ditches were brilliant with cow lilies, popsickle orange, a little bent on their long, graceful stems; beyond, in fields, the tall white yucca bloomed against the dingier cream of budding Queen Anne's lace. Pink clover and mauve thistles clustered exquisitely here and there, and going up the long hill I drove between lines of goldenrod, magnificent Edwardian heads still more green than yellow. Turning into our drive, I saw the house—as it seemed to me, for the first time—in its somber, homely, endearingly silly splendidness. The west windows blazed with afternoon light; shadows were thick beneath trees. Where the land dropped away at the back, the woods reared greenly. I had the sense of a penultimate moment; of apotheosis just before crisis. Braking as I coasted down toward the front porch, I thought of a dormitory that had burned during my years in college. The central section had been running with flames when the wings on either side were still tenanted. I remembered boys leaning out windows to crane round at the spectacle; electric lights were on, and curtains in a breeze moved back and forth over old sills. One saw pictures on walls, closet doors standing open to jumbles of robes and pajamas, jackets and coats and suits. Memory runs the scene through my mind in silence, but of course there must have been a ferocious uproar: the caving roof of the middle part, the walls coming down, the shouts of those of us who stood outside in front, the noise of the fire. But I can summon no sounds that seem right to me; it is all visual: the fire and the lights and the moving curtains, the juxtaposition of horror and domesticity that was briefly composed. Then, as if a siren had gone off, the tenants of the wings began throwing clothes, pillows, blankets, books, typewriters down onto the grass, and soon, pell-mell, were following themselves.

There were vast differences between that scene and this one; but what I chiefly felt were the similarities, and especially the moment's brilliance and the impossibility of its lasting—of something lasting, that is: our life, or its; I did not then know which.

Sarah was gone and the house empty, shining, smelling

just a little of the baby oil that Eleanor buys to treat furniture with. The awful humor struck me hard; this barren house fragrant with a children's preparation.

I went upstairs to the study, but at my desk I merely sat, scenes and conversations passing through my mind like an idle, nostalgic company. Eleanor and I were here on a visit, running through warm rain; I was a boy reading Poppy Ott on the library steps; I was spelling grandfather on the vast, hand-cranked ice-cream freezer, and from behind us, on the grass of the tennis court where trestle tables had been set up, came the murmur of the assembled family. Then we were in the woods, my sister and I and all our cousins, swinging on wild grapevines, balancing along fallen trunks, plucking bouquets of magnificent orange toadstools from decaying stumps, hunting morels in the damp springtime soil and puffballs in autumn.

The afternoon sun, dropping low, sent a harsher light into the room; shadows hardened and edges grew sharp. Above the bookcases all around me Axel Haig's engravings of cathedrals and their interiors showed a thin brownish bloom behind glass. Small foreground figures, dwarfed by flights of steps, by pillars and screens and windows, seemed to move, were about to move, at my glance froze back to rest. Alma, fixed in blazing light, came into my mind, burning white, pure, terrible. Then I thought of the fire, of walls coming down in flame while curtains moved gently. Panic danced toward me from a distance—so lightly, at first, that I scarcely attended its approach. Then up the steps it came, louder through the hard light, playing its jangling music.

Did I hear the girandole? Did carved wooden nails scratch their way over glittering floors?

I got up; sat down again. Absurd to be suddenly afraid, especially in this most familiar room—my one real sanctuary, here or anywhere else. Absurd. But it was perhaps its ordinariness that most played upon my mood: the horror lodged in the known, the customary: curtains and fire; Alma with murder burning brilliantly around her; this house with its restless tenant; my marriage, my wife, my child.

No, I couldn't write; I couldn't go on with our story now. I hauled myself upright once again and went downstairs—intentionally, by the back way. That was a coward's choice; and a fool's too, for I knew enough of its discretion to feel that it was in its usual place—that, in fact, it had really not moved since I'd capped it with the girandole. But I knew also that if I found it in the hall, or glimpsed it just vanishing back into the living room, I'd be seized by a trembling I wouldn't be able to control. I would shake apart, leaving the unhoused spirit helplessly to confront the patient, confident evil.

Had I eaten? When had I eaten? Coming into the kitchen, I was reminded that the day had gone: the clock stood at close to six. But several glasses of water filled me up, and then I had a double shot, neat. The whiskey gave me the smallest, the slightest of cheers. Hanging on the back of the basement door was Sarah's clothespin bag—though we have a drier, items such as sheets and towels regularly need the sun's bleaching, in Sarah's view. I dumped pins on the sink and put whiskey and a glass in their place. The metal loop of the bag I hooked over my waist, and with the rather bulky contents bumping against one hip I went outdoors and down the long kitchen flight.

Bound for where? Back to the pool? My imagination

balked at the familiar time-killer: stripping, swimming, dozing on a chaise, waking to find the sun gone and the moon riding the water. And so I descended without direction, as my legs carried me. Between the house and the tennis court stands a metal shed in which we store logs and branches intended for firewood or kindling. I remembered the small jobs I'd put between myself and a visit to Alma, earlier on this day. Chopping up kindling had been one of them. It came to me that by settling to something like this I was attesting to my faith in one or another kind of continuity at Owl Hill: my own, that of the two of us, that of the house . . . I didn't know. I was only certain that I wanted to believe in the supremacy of the life of this place over the evil that had moved out of the hills (as it seemed to me) and settled so confidently among us: that monstrous companion to death, vigilant, ironic, bold; full of resourcefulness and a horrible gaiety.

There was, of course, no ax. The shed leaks and any tool left inside would soon be furred with rust. But when had I used the ax last, and where had I put it down? In the basement, maybe?—beside the log waiter that carries firewood to the upper floors?

I was almost correct. Standing just inside the basement door, blinking to adjust to the dark, I saw presently the smallest, dullest of gleams. The ax was lying back in the waiter; I shouldn't have spotted it if I hadn't cleaned and oiled the blade quite recently, so that it caught the available light. I knelt sideways and groped—carefully, to avoid the cutting edge—and was a moment realizing that my fingers had closed round not the curved grip of the ax but someone's hand.

Flesh cool, firm, not resilient: I had had just enough

[ 187 ]

liquor and heat so that my reflexes signaled neither danger nor fear. I crouched there bemused at the impossibility of a hand in that particular space. Presently it moved, very slightly, drawing its fingers away from mine; it was gone, and beneath my touch was the surface of the ax handle. Cool, firm, not resilient; had I . . . ?

What was the ax doing in the waiter, anyway? It hadn't got there through my agency. Sarah?—in one of her periodic surveys of basement disorder? Eleanor rarely came down here, and never bothered with the tools, so it hadn't been she. The owner of the mysterious hand? There couldn't have been a hand, though, unless someone had been standing upside down in the shaft. I got the flashlight that's kept on top of the furnace and poked it inside the waiter, seeing, besides the ax, nothing except a few pieces of bark and some log dust. I turned the beam upward, but the shaft was empty; far above, on the second floor, I could make out a faint radiance from the door at that level, which someone had left open.

But no one could have scaled that height in the time it had taken me to react to the phenomenon; and even an effort to do so would have been too noisy to have gone unmarked.

I switched off the flash and, straightening up, took hold of the ax and drew it out. Could the handle possibly have felt like a palm, like fingers? No; never; and even supposing that for one improbable moment it had, what accounted for the sensation of withdrawal?

Then, only then, did a small fright possess me. I had immobilized the pedestal, apparently; but what agents could it muster to its business? What interest could it have in an ax?

The flesh across my neck and arms felt peculiarly exposed; familiar stretches of that vast basement were unwelcomely dark. Far off, in the old coal cellar, there was a scratching—a chipmunk got in, of course, or red squirrel, or even rat. But I thought of other clawed feet, wondered if the dark whirled round something tall, solid, that had first sent its agent ahead and then, horribly, come along itself, undeterred by the burden it carried.

Not casually, I backed toward the outside door and the sunlight. What made me swing round, offering my shoulders to the possible terror, was a cry or groan—so faint that my own footsteps almost extinguished it. There before me, for fully the blink of an eye, stood Ray. He was looking not at me but at the ax that unwittingly I still carried. I have no recollection of how he was dressed, but I know I could see the scar on his right thigh. The small noise came again; his arms spread out, hands cupped upward—but was the gesture beseeching or did it express resignation? Trembling uncontrollably, I stepped backward, and the ax fell from my hand to the concrete floor. At that, his eyes lifted; they passed across my face without recognition, rested briefly first here, and then there, beyond me.

He was gone.

# 35

AND THAT was how the kindling didn't get chopped, this day and forever more. I walked outdoors through the space where he had stood, shuddering, ready to flinch, but more appalled at the possibility that the light and the dark had even worse things to show if I stayed between them. At the shed I collected the clothespin bag and settled with it on a stone bench set under a tree some twenty feet farther down the slope, near the steps to the tennis court. It was as bad or as good a place as any to be; we had played checkers here sometimes, my sister and I, putting the scratched and dog-eared board between us, and I thought I remembered my grandmother, in a pale summer shawl, reading here in a small, thick book. It was the kind of place where a lady would read, a generation ago—or was it more strictly the kind of place where a lady might picturesquely pose? Had one's recollections got confused with the long-ago photograph or drawing accompanying a poem or an advertisement for something deeply refined? The real life of the past does so often yield to the conventional image of the placid, the extremely pretty, decorous yet joyful.

The day had got steadily hotter; the sky was overcast and the late sun had turned the cloud cover a dirty, livid yellow. I labored like a brave man over the contents of my bottle, soon abandoning the gentility of the cup, and I tried to think pleasantly of nothing: that is, of what my eyes wandered across, paused on: the mica that flashed in the stone seat whenever I made a slight movement; the baby squirrel on the shed roof, in doubt about leaping down, and then finally, legs spread wide, sailing into deep grass; a bramble of birds snarling across that yellow sky; and the house, the great porched and windowed, terraced and turreted house . . .

That was the trouble: the eye indifferently turned on many objects, but among them were some that roused the brain's articulation. An ax, a hand, a dead man with no business now in this place; a wife, a child—when had she come not to want our child? There was a time when we *had* tried to make one, both of us: no kindly onlooker would ever persuade me otherwise. We two alone had lived our marriage.

Where was she now? Not still at the doctor's. Seeking deviously for the help Ray had resisted giving her? Or wandering, in the way she'd done before: anything to keep out of the house? No.

No.

I was suddenly sure that she was meeting someone in the woods. I'd go look; I'd confront them both. She deserved to be shamed, punished. Her humiliation would be a pleasure! what a pleasure it would be!

Seized all at once by a rage that almost made me ill, I pushed myself upright, swayed a moment backward in space, my knees braced by the edge of the bench, and then aimed a course up the hill at a long angle that would bring me out on level lawn west of the house. I did not forget the bottle in the clothespin bag.

Bright red leaves; I'd see her brightly red, wounded by her own selfishness and cruelty. Red for punishment, for public notice: both were necessary.

The climb to the lawn so winded and dizzied me that twice I had to sit down, take a drink. Both times I looked around, stooped over the grass, seeing only grass, but seeing everything in my memory: What a beautiful place! What a pity it had to come to the people that we are. Something of our ugliness of spirit would always darken it, no matter what happiness came here later.

The pine grove was quiet, except for the clap of wings and the chutter of a dark bird that rose off a higher branch as I passed below. Here and there I could see the link fence bordering the western side of the property. The company that installed it and its twin to the east had told my grandfather he must keep them "clean"; otherwise their longevity couldn't be guaranteed. But for years trumpet vines had clambered along each—this was the season of their orange glory; and small-petaled, fast-falling dog roses also paced both lengths. The rope-vine poison ivy, too, unfortunately, still green now but later scarlet with noble white berries: no one had ever quite had the heart to kill it all.

All green; everything green, the red leaves transformed. Dodging, slipping, ducking, I went downhill into the hardwoods and found my windfall. From there I peered below. In glades, tall blue flowers like delphinium bloomed, and large plants with immense, jagged leaves supported gigantic blossoms as delicate and frail as morning-glories. All the greenery and the flowering confused me: where was it I had watched them, she hunched on herself, he standing at one side? I wasn't sure; perhaps at this ripe season I couldn't see far enough.

Amid such life and beauty, how had she brought herself to talk of the murder of our child? Determined, obsessive, she talked of it still, didn't she? She cared nothing for what lay round her. Oh, she was wicked, evil. Where was she? Who was with her?

I stumbled deeper into the woods, determined to find her out. Catching one foot in the hole of some animal, I sat firmly down, and rage and energy alike deserted me. Lying back on a wobbling elbow, I brought out the bottle, peered for a time in bafflement at what I finally recognized as the label, and turned it around until I had a clear view of the contents. The reddish-brown bourbon still was plentiful. I took a couple of long, satisfying drinks and then sank full-length on the leaf-packed ground. Green light ringed me; the air was fresh, the ground cool. I closed my eyes, and my last thought was: She's bound to die sooner or later; all of them are. It's foolish to . . . foolish . . .

Was that the real end, there in the summer woods, my drunken impotence and final stupefied confusion the pedestal's true objective? My objective, too, perhaps—the great thing with its claw feet being merely a projection of myself. The real end, all the actors gone, and night coming down.

But I am here once again, in this room. An hour ago, less, I stood before the house in brilliant moonlight that made the great windows on that north side dull, almost opaque. I had no memory of waking in the woods, staggering up and out onto the lawns; I had no recollection of waking or sleeping, of motion or rest. I was suddenly there before the immense, unlighted façade, under the huge white moon. A long-eared owl barked, then snarled like a cat; the air was full of wings and faint cries. Heat beat down, and no wind stirred, though from an upper window came a faint tap-tapping, as if a shade juttered in a draft.

It seemed urgent to me to possess my house, course it room by room, and passing into its shadow I climbed the broad, shallow steps to the porch and crossed to the front door. The dark consoled me, so once inside I didn't put on a light. Of course, I needed none; as I could walk the house in my mind, I could walk it in fact without touching a chair or table or door casing. So, at least, I believed.

I turned right into my grandfather's library, that alien room lately grown so familiar. Against the west window a cut-glass decanter filled with wine reflected the moon. On the same tray were several upended glasses, but I ignored these, and carrying the decanter I went back to the middle of the room and sank into a chair. Somewhere I had lost the bottle of bourbon in the clothespin bag. And I had that frantic thirst that heavy drinking induces.

The wine made me dizzy, though, and more than a bit ill; and after a few more hopeful swigs I put down the bottle and shut my eyes. But lights sprang up behind my lids, brilliant as flares; it was more restful to stare at the dark walls of books rising toward an invisible ceiling. The house ticked and sighed around me. I felt night occupying its immensity, jamming every room. And I felt also, quite suddenly, that this place was no longer mine. It had sloughed me off—I had no further part in its life, its absorptions, its future. The sensation brought not only panic, bad as that was, but a desolation so nearly absolute that lying back in the chair I could easily have surrendered my life; not just easily but gratefully. If the house, too, was lost to me, then I had nothing now at all. I wished there were someone to call, someone to ask to come and sit with me, drink with me. There was no one. Reviewing names, I felt vividly how much I was alone here—here and everywhere else as well. Oh, there were plenty of good people who would rally round in crisis; but where was the friend to whom I could say merely "Come," knowing my fright and desperation would be apprehended at once? To whom, of course, had I ever been such friend? I had no right, however great my longing, to expect what I myself had never given.

I realized that a glass of water was urgently necessary, and that I'd better make for the pitcher in the refrigerator. I pushed myself to the edge of the chair and after a moment, still sick and out of focus, got weakly to my feet. Swinging round, as I thought in the direction of the hall door, I hit a shin-high table. What table? What low table stood in this part of the room? The moon must have vanished, for absolute night swam around me. I was as lost and bewildered as one sometimes is groping from sleep to bathroom in clockless dark. Every surface I touched felt unfamiliar. Was I asleep? had I died minutes earlier in my despair? I moved sideways, struck something, a high-backed chair perhaps, knocked an ashtray or trinket off another table, and then collided with a wall. I groped along it, claustrophobic panic replacing other fears, subduing even thirst. In my imagination I tried to re-create the room, but nothing came to me except a jumble of images: and were they of this place or of somewhere else in the house?

I dropped to my knees and slowly crept along the wall. If only the moon would come out . . . Or was it still brilliantly lighted, the blackness confined just here—worse, just in me? My journey seemed interminable; the wall went on and on, never turning. My mouth burned; I felt increasingly dizzy, and had now and then to stop, rest my forehead against the floor. I *must* finally come to the door; beside the door was the light switch. Light would save me.

Then, somewhere near, I heard music; the chiming of the lusters. Ahead, I saw a faint glow. Somehow, it seemed, I had got into the hall. I drew myself up, uncertain whether to go forward or back into the revolving dark. But I knew of course that I couldn't do that; that this was the hour, this the confrontation. The pedestal commanded my house, commanded me.

What could it do, after all?—what could it do that hadn't been done to me already? Why fear it? It might even offer some release. It alone seemed concerned to penetrate my isolation, to involve me in whatever its terrible vitality was directed toward.

The glow became steadily brighter at a speed not in ratio to my steps and trembling pauses. I could make out the staircase at my left, the little table on which the girandole had stood, the flanking chairs. I reached the door to the living room, and then for a long time I stuck, my head against the casing, my eyes defensively closed. I had no will to draw me backward, no strength to go inside. But the music grew louder, composed itself into a melody that was irresistible, so sad and strange and wild. In my brain the lusters danced, the moon bowled through one and then another and then set them all to burning. The pedestal swayed, sighed, flexed its claws so sharply I seemed to feel them scoring my neck and back. Voices spoke to me, called out my name; the music sank to a murmur and then rose again, more compelling, more heartbreaking than ever.

Did the hand take mine and lead me forward? I thought so; I thought I was drawn into the room. There I saw that after all the pedestal and I were no longer by ourselves.

My wife had come home.

Her head was neatly skewered on the tall spearlike finial of the girandole. She regarded me without interest, as perhaps she had always done in her essential self. The ragged flesh of her severed neck dangled among the flashing lusters, a few of which were darkly spotted, perhaps with blood. So our long quest was ended; she was the perfect finish to the pedestal, the child of inspiration that we'd sought.

On the floor lay the ax, badly stained; no one would ever want to use it again. Beside it was a clothespin bag in which a bottle of bourbon was partly visible.

My wife's mouth dropped open, as if she had a last thing to say, but all that came out was a little bit of red that drew itself crookedly down her chin.

The pedestal moved.

# 36

I AM at my desk; it hasn't ever been able to get upstairs. With that burden of crystal and flesh, it can't possibly make the climb. But I can hear it singing, singing, somewhere in the hall near the stairs; it has got that far. Singing, and calling me; they are all calling me. And at the window wings are beating, and fingers tap gently. An owl shouts. Is it tomorrow that Sarah will run from the house, down the hill into the woods? As I turn toward the music, toward the rush and sigh, toward their voices, I ask myself what she'll see here? Dear God, what wonder, what strangeness, what magnificence of the terrible will she find?